W9-CEJ-644

Grand Fathers

OTHER HOLT TITLES BY NIKKI GIOVANNI

The Genie in the Jar
illustrated by Chris Raschka

Grand Mothers

Shimmy Shimmy Shimmy Like My Sister Kate

The Sun Is So Quiet
illustrated by Ashley Bryan

Grand Fathers

Reminiscences, Poems, Recipes,
and Photos of the Keepers
of Our Traditions

Edited by
Nikki Giovanni

Henry Holt and Company • *New York*

Henry Holt and Company, Inc.
Publishers since 1866
115 West 18th Street
New York, New York 10011

Henry Holt is a registered
trademark of Henry Holt and Company, Inc.

Collection copyright © 1999 by Nikki Giovanni
All rights reserved.
Published in Canada by Fitzhenry & Whiteside Ltd.,
195 Allstate Parkway, Markham, Ontario L3R 4T8.

Library of Congress Cataloging-in-Publication Data
Grand fathers: reminiscences, poems, recipes, and photos of
the keepers of our traditions / edited by Nikki Giovanni.
p.   cm.
Summary: A collection of varied tributes to grandfathers,
reflecting their special roles in families.
1. Grandfathers—literary collections. [1. Grandfathers—Literary collections.]
I. Giovanni, Nikki.
PZ5.G6953   1999   810.8'03520432—dc21   98-38463

ISBN 0-8050-5484-7
First Edition—1999
Printed in the United States of America on acid-free paper. ∞
1 3 5 7 9 10 8 6 4 2

Grateful acknowledgment is made for permission to reprint the following:
"The Satisfaction Coal Company" by Rita Dove is excerpted from *Thomas and Beulah*.
Copyright © 1986 by Rita Dove. Reprinted by permission of the author.
"Grandpop's Macaroni and Cheese" is from *Downhome Wholesome* by Danella Carter.
Copyright © 1995 by Danella Carter. Used by permission of Dutton,
a division of Penguin Putnam, Inc.
"Papa's Fresh Beet Horseradish" is from *Beni's Family Cookbook for the Jewish Holidays*
by Jane Breskin Zalben. Copyright © 1996 by Jane Breskin Zalben,
published by Henry Holt and Company, Inc.
All other entries are copyright the individual author or artist.

*To all the men who didn't hit their wives,
kick their dogs, or holler at their children and
threaten to leave if they weren't ready on time*

Contents

◉◉◉

WAS TOO TALL FOR THE SHELF

SO IT STOOD

NINETY YEARS ON THE FLOOR

BUT IT STOPPED . . . SHORT

The Warm Hearth Writers' Workshop

Grand Fathers

We Came Together:
In Praise of Grandfathers

Grandfathers are notes. Songs that we sing. Not all the songs are happy songs. Not all the songs are good songs. Songs don't have to be good, after all, to be sung. They just have to be known. Grandfathers are not little dots that we sing along to. The bouncing ball does not call up a grandfather name that the audience shouts out as if he were a jolly good fellow. Grandfathers are not uncles or brothers or cousins who can kick the can or play perfect mumblety-peg. Not all grandfathers are jolly good. Some do laugh aloud. Some do tell tales. Some, though, are silent. For the silence of love that gentles the heart and makes the voice stick in the throat. For the silence of love that makes the wishes on the stars already burdened with too much of the world's troubles. Grandfathers have seen it all. The wars and the weapons of war. The hurts and the harm of hate. Grandfathers hope for us. Wish for us. Sing our song. Cross their fingers that they were good fathers. Cross their fingers that they will be better grandfathers. Looking at the calluses on their hands and in their hearts, know they have done a splendid job at both.

My mother's father, whom we called Grandpapa, was twenty years the senior of Grandmother. He was a Fisk University graduate who had named his first daughter Yolande. We often wondered about that. If Grandpapa graduated in 1905, then W. E. B. DuBois had not already named his daughter, who would later marry Countee Cullen, Yolande. We had always thought it was his admiration for DuBois that made him choose that name. Recently, in corresponding with David DuBois, we learned that they both had a Spanish teacher named Yolande and that most likely she was the reason they both had daughters with a romantic name. It's funny, isn't it, that after all these years we have become curious about something that now cannot be answered? I wonder why it never came up before. Why didn't I sit next to his chair and say, "Grandpapa, why did you name Mommy Yolande?" Since he loved to tell stories, he would have turned to me and started, "Well, you know . . ." and that mystery would have been solved.

He used to love to talk about his almost diplomatic career. He would read something in the papers and he'd say, "Now, if I had been ambassador . . ." and I would be amazed. This man whose kitchen I was sitting in could have been in all those places and done all those wonderful things for world peace, for the protection of liberty, for the betterment of the entire planet. The Nobel Peace Prize–winner Ralph Bunche and those guys never impressed me all that much, because my grandfather could have done so much more. And would have been so humble about it. "Well," he would say, "I would have resolved the Suez blockade by . . ." or "I would have told Ben-Gurion . . ." or "I would have made the Kaiser . . ."—"if I hadn't met your grandmother." No wonder people think grandmothers are so powerful. Luckily for the third rock from the yellow sun, there were people around who didn't meet my grandmother, so they did the work of the world while Grandpapa taught Latin at Austin High.

Mama Dear, Cornelia Watson, my great-grandmother, was born a free child of slave parents. I don't know much about Mama Dear. She was very old when I met her and she died shortly thereafter. My mother talks about Mama Dear, and my grandmother always spoke so fondly of her it took me a long time to realize that Mama Dear was Grandpapa's mother, not Grandmother's. When Grandpapa married Grandmother, her mother died, and Grandmother always thought that God sent Mama Dear to take her mother's place. Grandpapa had three daughters and a wife, and his mother lived with them for the rest of her life. He was surrounded by females, and it was to the good of us all. Grandpapa's idea of temper was "Oh, my!"

We all scattered when we heard that. I never knew him to interfere with anything Grandmother was saying or doing with us grandchildren, but late at night you could catch bits of "Do you think you should have made them come back in just because . . . ?" "Well, John Brown, I don't want their mothers to come back for their little bodies. . . ." And the classical dialogue between dreams and safety would ensue. Grandpapa's voice was always on an even keel. Grandmother would fly off the handle, would shout at you, would laugh so hard she could shake the house, but Grandpapa was always just calm. He could radiate delight, he certainly did laugh, and his displeasure was easily known, yet I have no memory of any radical changes in his approach to things. Perhaps Grandpapa was simply never frustrated. He knew what he thought, what he felt, what he could and could not do, so that the energy that fuels frustration and violence never had the opportunity to seep into his heart.

Grandpapa did the shopping. He was built like his mother, Mama Dear, lean, strong. He walked uptown from Mulvany Street to Gay Street, which was then the heart of Knoxville. He shopped the market for whatever Grandmother needed. But he always brought gingerbread men back for us. Grandmother would say, "John Brown, you're just spoiling those children!" And he would say, "Now, Mother . . ." And we would have great big gingerbread men with ruby eyes made out of the stuff they make minced meat from. You could chew them from the legs to the arms to the middle, then pick the eyes out—because, at least in my case, I hate minced-meat anything, including pie, fruitcakes, and any of those kinds of things—then start at the top and eat the head. One of the truly sad culinary days for me was when people quit making gingerbread men by hand; the other was when they quit stirring fudge. Some things require a human being. Like ice cream.

My grandfather made the very best ice cream in the world. I do remember Saturdays, when the iceman would come by and we would get twenty-five pounds of ice. It would go in a tub with burlap wrapped around it. It was fascinating. Like a big diamond. Grandpapa made the custard on Saturday nights. Six eggs (beaten), two cups sugar, one quart milk, one pint whipping cream, one tablespoon vanilla. Grandpapa cooked his custard, skimming the top, then, when it cooled, strained it through cheesecloth and put it in the refrigerator to cool. Their refrigerator was the old-fashioned kind without a true freezer, just that little slit at the top. I don't remember when they bought a big refrigerator with a big freezer, but I remember always loving that old one, which, if I had been old enough with sense enough to keep it, would now be some sort of antique. Grandmother's favorite ice cream was peach. When peaches were in season Grandpapa would dip them in boiling water, pop the skin off, cut them up, and let them sit in sugar until he was ready to churn the next day.

Grandmother almost always cooked Sunday dinner on Saturday night, so that after church we only had to wait for the rolls to be baked. I don't know why, and as far as I know no one else does either, but Grandpapa had to have hot bread with each meal. If Grandmother had gone to a lodge meeting or to some of the other out-of-town obligations she had taken on, Grandpapa would cook. But the two things he had to have in order for a meal to seem right were hot bread and dessert. Sometimes they were the same thing, because he would make dessert out of toast with Alaga syrup over it. We always loved it but it was funny to see him very patiently making this rather strange meal for us. He also would toast his cereal in the morning, though he put cold milk on it. He must have informed my culinary tastes more than I realized, since I heat my crackers and potato chips and microwave my olives.

Grandpapa loved the stars. Maybe because of his love of Latin and Greek myths, maybe because of his love of learning, but he loved the stars. He would tell stories about Orion's belt; the Big Dipper; he would point out The Twins. He would stand on his front porch on clear nights and tell about constellations and why they were named as they were. He always told a good story, though never the guffaw kind, never the punch line, but always the educational point, always the uplifting parable. Grandfathers are songs we sing. I know fathers are important, because without them we could never have grandfathers. But I think it's fair to say grandfathers are the best of fathers.

Our book *Grand Mothers* deserves a companion, and we created *Grand Fathers*. I wanted to look at this oak tree, this steady stream, this flow through wind, this breeze who makes up our grandfathers. This collection is not definitive. It is not all grandfathers. But it does show us the mostly good, sometimes not-good person we love. It does help awaken us to the heart of the old man who always seemed to get the first hot biscuit, the first slice of Sunday roast beef, the baseball game he wanted on the radio, the television show he wanted whether or not he held the remote. Grandfathers rule with a deep respect for grandmothers. Which is probably why they get their way. I hope this collection will encourage young people to solve some of their families' mysteries. I hope that the young will ask questions and listen to answers spoken and unspoken.

We came together to show that grandfathers, like grand-mothers, are universal to the human experience. That it takes time and work and heart and soul to be a good grand-father. That grandfathers are of all colors and all races and all religions but actually one race and one color and one reli-gion: human, human, and human.

We came together in this gaggle of grandfathers to take a look at how the fathers had matured. Fathers who would never admit mistakes apologize to grandsons; fathers who belittled daughters praise granddaughters; fathers who strayed from the homefires are content to sit with grand-mothers and recall earlier times. Grandfathers are a good vintage wine, an excellent aged steak, single-malt scotch that is all golden in the bottle. Open a father and a great grandfather whiffs his way into our lives. We are constantly amazed that fathers whom we had grown to dislike became charming men whose company we actually seek. We look at the grandfathers who stayed home; we look at the grand-fathers who tried to build a mansion of the heart with many rooms to wander in; we look at grandfathers who are silent though loving. Some of our grandfathers didn't come through. One grandfather found his hatred more important than his progeny; one grandfather was skipping out on Grandmother and it is the grandson who has to tell him, "Cut that out!" Grandfathers are like the rest of us who are struggling to make sense of this world. They are the tears we shed. They are who we turn to when something bothers us. They are the stars we wish upon, for it is grandfathers, I believe, more than any other males, who let us see what loving relation-ships should be.

MY GRANDFATHER'S CLOCK

John Harvey Bigelow
(1875–1977)

Jessie Carney Smith

The most fascinating man I have ever known was my maternal grandfather, John Harvey Bigelow. He was proud and humble, firm but not overbearing, religious but religiously tolerant, respected and respectful, and as honest as anyone needed to be. A landowner and small farmer, he was well known in Guilford County and surrounding areas in North Carolina, where he spent a lifetime. I am proud to be one of his descendants.

John Harvey Bigelow, whom I knew as "Granddad," was born on June 15, 1875, in Caswell County, North Carolina, some twenty miles from Yanceyville. He grew up in the Sweet Gum community, which may have been his birthplace. His date and place of birth are documented in the U.S. census records for 1900 and in the family Bible that he kept. His mother, Fannie Harvey Bigelow, a mulatto, was born in the 1820s and died in the early 1900s, when she was about ninety-five years old. She married Henry Harvey, and after his death she married a man named Bigelow. Never a slave,

JOHN HARVEY BIGELOW

Fannie Harvey was a house servant and cook for a white family named Rascoe. Though undocumented, it is said that Louis Rascoe—a brother to the head of the Rascoe family—was Granddad's father; Granddad, however, assumed or was given the surname of his mother's husbands. Louis Rascoe and his wife, Lou Susan Rascoe, had several other sons, all half-brothers to my grandfather. One of them, Preston, was a druggist in the area. I recall seeing some of the Rascoe descendants when they came to visit my grandparents when I was a child. Granddad looked a lot like some of them; he was tall, lanky, and fair-skinned. He had gray eyes and wiry straight hair. Family legend said little about the matter, and Granddad barely spoke of that part of his life to my mother and her siblings.

Some of the stories, however, are interesting and curious. Granddad must have been born a saint. He was deeply religious and probably never broke a law—God's or man's.

Granddad's universe was at first Caswell County. Apparently he was highly respected in the area, both by blacks and whites. The story goes that he was a carpenter by trade. The 1900 Census lists Granddad as a laborer on a Rascoe farm in Caswell County. When he was a young, unmarried man, he agreed to work with a local white man for one dollar a week for a year, after which he was to be paid. When the twelve months passed, the contractor owed him fifty dollars, since two dollars had been used for the sale of two pigs that Granddad bought for his mother. Repeated efforts to collect his pay were ignored. After all, this was in the rural South in the late nineteenth century, where whites took whatever liberties with blacks they deemed appropriate. Granddad would take it no longer; with him a deal was a deal, what was fair was fair, and race did not make an acceptable exception. He contacted Filian Dillard, the local sheriff, who knew clearly that John Bigelow was Louis Rascoe's son and a fair and honest man as well. The sheriff ordered the bill paid! Then Granddad was paid in full in gold pieces. In his comments about the episode, Granddad rejoiced: "I was the richest nigger in Caswell County."

By Granddad's account, he was the best baseball pitcher in Caswell and nearby counties. He belonged to a local team which had both black and white players. Although Granddad was a fast runner as well, one of his team members, Lawson Morgan, was faster and therefore at times was his designated runner. The racial segregation of Alamance County in the late nineteenth century made no difference to the white players; they would not begin a game unless their star pitcher, John Bigelow, was present.

The young, tall, handsome man must have been considered a fine catch in his community. While in his twenties, he met what he considered the prettiest woman he had ever seen. Their courtship led to a marriage proposal to Minnie Magnolia Lea, of Mebane, North Carolina, who would become my grandmother. Grandma set a new mark for blacks in the area. For her impending marriage she sent wedding invitations announcing the event—an unheard-of act for blacks, at least in Granddad's Caswell County. Among those attending the wedding in late December 1900 were the best man and baseball-team player from Caswell County, Lawson

Morgan; and Grandma's cousin and maid of honor, Martha Brown, from Alamance County. The Bigelows and Morgans remained friends until Lawson Morgan died, only four months before Granddad celebrated his one hundredth birthday in June 1975. Martha Brown was present at the birthday celebration. A wedding gift from the minister who performed the ceremony, a beverage set, remains a treasured possession in my family.

Grandma and Granddad first lived in a farmhouse on the Rascoes' property in Caswell County, where Granddad continued to work as a carpenter and farmer while Grandma went about having children. An outspoken man, Granddad had no difficulty saying what he thought was right. Concerning his work on the farm, a local white farmer asked, "John, how much help do you have?" Granddad replied, "Just myself." "Doesn't your wife work?" the other man asked, expecting that all black women worked the farm with their husbands. "No, does yours?" Granddad replied.

Though he had limited education, having attended only a few grades in a one-room school in Caswell County, Granddad wanted the best education he could afford for his children. There would be six eventually—all girls, born on average two years apart, from 1901 to 1914. Granddad knew that Greensboro, some forty-five miles away in Guilford County, had a much better school system for blacks than Caswell County. In addition to high schools, Greensboro had two black colleges—Bennett and the state-owned Agricultural and Technical College of North Carolina.

About 1908, Granddad moved his family by horse and buggy to a farm some three and a half miles east of Greensboro. He moved his family into what had been a hotel or an overnight stop for weary travelers while he worked as a farmhand for white landowner Will Fry, who had a sizable farm. But Granddad had set his sights on owning his own farm, which he achieved about 1911. His nineteen-acre farm and house were located about a mile east of the Fry place. Now he was on his way to independence. Grandma, who rarely worked on the farm, drove a horse and buggy to Greensboro to sell fruit, vegetables, and butter to local residents. Their daughters were educated in Greensboro, all six receiving a college education. With one exception, they became teachers in the public schools. Although he never learned to drive, Granddad purchased a car for his daughters' transportation to school. My mother, now ninety-four, and two of her sisters survive.

Although Granddad became a very religious man, in his early life he was not a member of any church. He grew up in his mother's church, which he called Sweet Gum, a Baptist church in Caswell County. He never believed that other churches could compare to Sweet Gum, by his standards the world's number-one house of religion. Nor did his love for Caswell County diminish over the years. After his move to Guilford County, his religious upbringing took hold, and in 1908 he became a founder of Laughlin Memorial Methodist Episcopal Church in the Mount Zion community, located about two miles west of his community. As was customary in Granddad's younger days, church functions were the leading social outlets for blacks. Popular among such functions were revival meetings. These were often held in peaceful outdoor areas. Granddad loved the revivals and attended those in nearby areas when he could. At Laughlin he made barrels of lemonade for the annual Children's Day celebrations held in June. We looked forward to the best lemonade we ever had. Granddad also held various positions in the church: treasurer, Sunday-school superintendent, and Sunday-school teacher. He and his close friend Albert Troxler were near the same age and both important in church leadership.

Granddad enjoyed his small community, his farm, his family, and his racial mix of friends. After his crops were planted in spring and before harvest time, he made batches of locust beer as well as apple cider (which we knew included worms, dirt, and the works). Those who knew him often came by for a drink of either beer or cider. In late summer he cooked a regional dish called Brunswick stew, to which he added a variety of vegetables, meats, and wild game, prepared outdoors in a cast-iron pot. He invited neighbors in for an early-evening feast. Often they brought vegetables or meats to add to the stew. At night he played cards with the men in the community, in either his home or theirs.

The farm provided an abundance of fresh fruits and vegetables—the prettiest, I thought, that ever grew. He must have been a master gardener. I never saw tomatoes so big, so red; beans so bountiful; watermelons in such full supply. Granddad had a sizable patch of cantaloupes and watermelons, to which we helped ourselves after nightfall, when he had retired for the day. We also knew to avoid the big melons, for Granddad would miss them; he would pull them later and serve them to what our aunt Oves called "Granddad's white people." To Granddad, race was never an issue, yet we thought he saved the best for them. We knew that on Sundays whites would visit him to feast on his melons. Granddad also gathered the family to eat his melons, which we much enjoyed. After canning season, Grandma gave their visitors her best and prettiest jars of canned fruit and vegetables.

Granddad shopped for groceries on Saturdays and walked about two miles to "Miz Story's" or Blalock's Grocery Store, in the Bessemer area, to do the shopping. He also did odd jobs for Miz Story, who sometimes drove him home in her car or had someone else do so.

In my youth, Granddad always seemed to be the tallest and oldest man I knew. My siblings and I loved walking to Sunday school or to the grocery store with him, although we could never keep up with him. We also looked forward to the treats he bought us.

Granddad celebrated his one hundredth birthday on June 15, 1975, at the home of his daughter Oves, where he and Grandma lived their later years. (Grandma had died five years earlier.) On the eve of his birthday, Granddad, anxious about the occasion and fearing he might actually die from excitement, asked to be awakened at midnight. He wanted to be certain that he would, in fact, reach his one hundredth birthday. After that he returned to bed until early morning. The *Greensboro Daily News* for June 16 published his photo-

graph and an interview with the centenarian. He told the re-
porter, "It's God's will that I have lived this long . . . but I
think I might have had something to do with getting the
Lord to will what he has." He spoke of his experience as a
young man, just before the turn of the century, doing many
odd jobs for two old ladies who lived in his community. "But
the Bible says to honor your father and mother and that, if
you do, your days may be long. I reckon honoring your father and mother means to honor the elderly too." He took
pride in describing his lifetime diet, one that would cause
nutritionists some consternation: "I've never eaten greens or
leafy vegetables. I've stuck to sweets: butter, milk, molasses,
pies and honey." He had defied the warning a family friend
gave his mother years earlier, that "that boy won't live to get
grown" because of his poor and skimpy diet. Martha Brown,
who had attended his wedding, came early to join in his
birthday celebration. So did Albert Troxler and his white
friend Charlie Clapp. All in this group were ninety years or
more themselves. They shared the morning with Granddad
and enjoyed hearing the conversations about baseball in the
previous century, the events of 1900, and vegetable gardening. That afternoon, younger guests came. Granddad was
proud to show his visitors the birthday greeting he had
received from President Gerald Ford and clutched it most of
the day. The occasion was the most exciting one I have ever
witnessed.

As well loved and respected as Granddad was, there were
times when race and tradition interfered with his ability to
receive the honor and respect due such a proud, honest, de-

serving, and religious black man. The story goes that his former employer Will Fry asked Granddad if Grandma could sit with his wife, who was ill; Granddad remarked: "I'll ask her if she wants to and if she says yes I'll let her go this time. But if you want yourself somebody, you'd better get yourself somebody." Grandma simply was not to work outside the home for anyone! I became irritated when young whites especially, and their parents, called him "John," or, worse yet, "Uncle John." He was not their uncle. And he was Mr. Bigelow! He called the adults Mr. Charlie, Miz Blalock, or whatever their names were. I also resented his going to the back doors of white people's homes to knock and enter; they always came to his front door! Granddad never discussed these practices or appeared to resent them, nor was he ever a lackey. Later, I understood the racism of the time, but I still resented the lack of respect that I knew he was given.

Granddad was certainly no Uncle Remus, but the animals seemed to treat him with great respect. His horse Mollie seemed to do whatever he said, whether he worked her on the farm or rode her, which he did on few occasions. He enjoyed the outdoors. A precision shooter, he loved to hunt and was always highly successful, whether hunting quail, rabbits, or squirrels. People came from miles around to hunt with Granddad or have him train their dogs to hunt. He also trained his own dogs well, and he and his bird dogs and beagles loved each other deeply.

I think God respected Granddad, too. When he spoke, people listened, whether my father, the black community, white people, or the family. He had tremendous respect for

Grandma, and for women generally. As I reflect on his life, I think he was never a chauvinist, but he was a man of great determination.

Granddad was a great storyteller. He told appealing tales—some true, some fable—of being the best baseball pitcher in Caswell County; of animals, even eels; of experiences with his mother. He fascinated little children in our family with his stories, and with his fake tears when he wanted to prove a point.

I never knew him to drink alcohol or, until his last days, to visit a doctor. He rolled his own cigarettes and especially cigars and smoked a pipe, but gave up smoking abruptly when he was about seventy. He had his own remedies for the few illnesses he encountered; for example, to treat a cold he took small amounts of kerosene with sugar. He also never swore. But his favorite word used to express disgust was "dadgummit." He walked everywhere, accepting rides in cars only when he had to. Wherever he went, he was certain to return home before dark, primarily because he believed a family man should be at home at night. In his house there was Granddad's chair, Granddad's plate, Granddad's cup and glass, as well as the same items for Grandma. Grandma had a swing and Granddad a hammock. His standard dress at home included a shirt, tie, and jacket or cardigan sweater.

We enjoyed having breakfast with our grandparents on Sunday morning. Granddad always said an especially long prayer, after which we had a hearty meal. Of course we had plenty of food at my parents' house nearby, but there was something special about Sunday mornings with our grandparents. Granddad loved his grandchildren, especially my two brothers, most especially my twin, Jodie. Jodie could do no wrong, and Granddad spoiled him rotten. He never exploited us as a source of child labor; he always paid us for our work with him on his tobacco farm.

Over the years, Granddad kept abreast of world events by reading the local newspaper and sporadically listening to the radio; when the news was over, he turned the set off to save electricity. Concerning the space program, at first he doubted that man had ever reached the moon. Then he conceded that man had, but, as many other older people believed, said that "we had no business up there" and that "the weather has never been right since."

When he was ninety-two, Granddad gave up gardening. He walked throughout the community visiting friends and shut-ins; friends also visited him. He crossed a busy highway to chat for hours with Pettis West, a blind white man who operated a pottery shop in the community; then our family ordered him to stay away from the highway. After Grandma died at age ninety-five (they were only three months apart in age), he survived without a lot of obvious grief. Little mattered much at this stage of his life. At the age of ninety-eight, he often read the local newspaper without his drugstore eyeglasses, because he could not find them and could see without them anyway. He had difficulty walking, though, and his hearing was failing. Seeing him struggle with a walker was painful. Still, he struggled on. After a physician friend offered to fit him for prescription eyeglasses and a hearing aid to help improve the quality of his life when he was about ninety-seven or ninety-eight, Granddad refused: "No, sir! I've seen all I want to see and heard all I want to hear."

When infirmities of old age caught up with him, he was hospitalized for a few days, and died peacefully on Friday, February 4, 1977, in L. Richardson Memorial Hospital, a black facility in Greensboro. He was buried in a family plot at Laughlin Memorial Church's cemetery.

Coda

🌀🌀🌀

Nikky Finney

We are four to a bed   So close our hips must come with
hinges   A ticking of brown family thrown across the cotton
and feather mattress   Tucked deep inside the house my
grandfather raised up from the red earth straight into the
wooly air

    The black and white photograph isn't supposed to predict
the future   But my mother looks like my unborn brother
And even at three I am different   My tiny black girl eyes are
a queer shade of green   At five my older brother stands there
on the end already buttoned into my father's sense of place

    We are so close in this cherry bed   Our lightly touching
hips must surely be hinged   Even the children have them
Daddy has moved into his place next to Mama   Mama has
moved in next to me   I am the only one who has a wall
The whole house has fallen asleep but me   The movie is
about to begin

    Uncle Billy is just home from Vietnam   He is the baby
He stands before us with a new camera that the war bought

for him   I call Uncle Billy *The Bonneville Man*   Just like
Pop Leo he can fix anything   Unlike him he will only drive
a car if it's pretty

Thirty years later *The Bonneville Man* will die of AIDS
alone in another bed without hinges   A dozen headlights
polka dot the night screen wall   Every long pretty car he
ever owned drives by to pay its last respects   He snaps the
picture of us all and horns blow out in a scatter like blue
Cadillac whales

We are a charm bracelet of a family bedding down for the
night in the outback of my mother's country   We have been
laid flat for the sake of photography   The elder aborigines
bump from room to rafter watching us amazed   They whisper how much we resemble early black and white TV

By midnight more of us have joined more of us   We lop
around the old four poster in a three dimensional ring like a
black family cutout doll   We are joined at the hip inside the
old homehouse   We have been hinged together in a place
pulled from the ribs of ancient Indian land called Newberry

We are Southern North American Africans   Whenever
we sleep together the rubbing together of our bones makes
for a better crop   Daddy's hipbone clickclacks into place
next to Mama   And a new brother seven years and ten
pounds away from birth snuggles in next to me

The new tenant brother takes up space I thought was all
mine   But Mama says not to move him   She says he is the
last one   She tells me what I already know   He will always
need more of her than me   The Silver Queen has already
been harvested   The second reel begins

Somebody down the road is passing a new baby over a fresh grave packed with seashells   The simmering dust is spinning off the blue corn silk   An ocher wind pattycakes the glass until dawn   I know better than to sing along Mama would only turn and shush me   Tell me to stop playing with myself

That is why I always sleep by the wall   For company So the movie will have a screen   So the screen will have a witness   Now all I have to do is live   Big brother there on the end turns and I follow tumbling in an arc along with him   Our hinges shift but never open   These are the first days that my feet and body begin to leave the floor without warning   There is a white dog out in the woods howling

Pop Leo will shoot him between the eyes tomorrow then drag him back to the clearing near the arrowhead ground He will never explain to me what madness is and how we all can go   I am the only one still awake to see the end For twenty years something or someone will come and lift me all the way up to the ceiling and back whenever it wants   I will come to know this as primordial brown girl levitation

The black snakes are tunneling under the hay in the barn for warmth   I see the mice go still in terror at the long dragon vessels nearing   They are born knowing they can be swallowed whole   Like them I have wondered how long it takes to die when you are eaten and made to watch

I am counting practicing my numbers   At the cow trough that Pop built fifty years ago with heavy two handed pieces of limestone   The spigot is dripping nineteen drops

per minute   Eleven   Twelve   Fifteen   I work hard on
learning my numbers in case there is ever a test   The water
drops fall all night   Even though I used two hands to shut
it off just like I was told

Except for the howling of something white farther off in
the woods that has lost someone it resembles   I am attached at the waist to my brothers by my mother but I know
I am free to fly   I am a lee little long legged girl   A southern mixture of giraffes and red velvet rice and everything
nice   I have no memory of winter as a child

A peacock is still something I have never seen before
But in two hours over breakfast Aunt Willa will lie and say
she has   And her sapphire words will glitter like a tickling
rain rolling off the curly tin roof of the barn   I will see
them leave her mouth and hit the frying air like that of a
howling dog or a torpedoing snake

I will remember last spring at the county fair when she
slithered toward us waving her turquoise green tongue like
a fan of exotic feathers   I do not remember if Daddy snored
back when we slept in this warm ring of soft brown bones
And only now do I understand that my random levitations
and landings had to do with four little girls from
Birmingham and a bomb

The all night rubbing of bones has turned the inside tips
of my fingers alabaster   Someone has dusted the homemade
cotton sheets on both sides with self-rising flour   I need
someone to help hear the many broken whispers coming
through the walls up from the land where the dead skin of
my grandfather dropped for years like seed

I always wanted a sister   Another girl to remember the land would be nice   She could help rewind the film back onto the reel   Like shelves of brown encyclopedias Pop Leo's arms always knew the answer to everything   No visible timepieces were ever kept in this house that he built and she made   Just so we would never think of leaving

Any minute I will smell her perfect fig biscuits and he will pour his black coffee out of his cup and into his saucer He will drop his full Cherokee lips to the cool rim then tilt himself back in a sip   As the babylight comes inviting the day I hear him wishing his throat was a mile long   Finally I am falling

I am the only girl   I know the hinges we have worn all night made of soft shell salmon bones will fall away at the first shock of light   I know when the rooster finally steps it will be like High John the Conqueror into the morning broom swept yard

I know only then will we unhook as a mule team and one by one make our way into the ice box bathroom where in the face bowl an image will appear and we will wash our privates by ourselves

Poppa

❧❧❧

Sterling Plumpp

I was born sixty years before I was born and I wrote poems fifty years before I was born. I am someone raised from birth until I am fifteen by maternal grandparents. Therefore I was born January 26, 1880, when my grandfather was born, and I became a poet on January 8, 1890, when my grandmother was born. Poppa, what I call my grandfather, Victor Emmanuel, went home to ancestors on January 8, 1955, and Momma, what I call my grandmother, Mattie Emmanuel, went home on November 23, 1993, after 103 years of witnessing. My existence begins with the birth of my grandfather; his beginning is mine.

His life bridges the gap between slavery and African-American determination to move from backseats. Born just four years prior to the greatest lynching interval (1884–1900), when it is reported that two thousand five hundred blacks were lynched, he died in January of the year the Montgomery Boycott began. My grandfather's life was fought, searched for, defined, and won in that bloody interlude between the Civil War and the arrival of the end of Jim Crow.

My idea of language comes from the cadences of his voice beseeching the Lord to spare him, his wife, and grand-chilluns during the intensity of storms that caused the shacks to shake. It comes from his voice thanking the "heavenly Father" for seeing him through another night and giving him another day. His voice in prayer was the very first blues I heard. Poppa is how I addressed him and how I remember him. This short, humpbacked, intense black man set the boundaries of my imagination. He wore his manhood like a tailored suit. A grandfather is not a father substitute; he is a way of life, a history, a culture, and a memory.

When I think back I cannot but marvel that the small dark man that was my grandfather rooted me in a sense of history and a sense of myth. I knew he had short breath and often stopped for a while as we neared the end of a row when chopping cotton, or plowing, or picking cotton. I know that sometimes I thought he would cough up his lungs or liver. I knew there were signs in him all my life which spelled death. Yet, the stories he told about the happenings at cotton gins had power. I learned very early the meaning of the anecdote, the space it created in my life, how it is woven and rewoven: Criss Cross opened his mouth too wide at the cotton gin. When Mr. Reynolds, who supplied all the tenants, stated that the bale weighed such and such, Criss simply said, "The scales say it weighs two hundred pounds more." For this indiscretion, Ben Light slapped him in the face. Thus Criss Cross bore a triple burden: he had been cheated by the boss man, slapped by a white intermediary, and had to ride seventy miles in the back of a truck driven by the man who had slapped him. Nobody said a word while they drove.

Poppa was a bundle of paradoxes: he could display genuine kindness and abrupt shifts to anger. When Henry threw water on his youngest daughter and her sister, Carrie shot him and fled home. Poppa met Henry bleeding in the road and gave him money to get to a doctor and told him if he ever saw him again he would kill him. White men might rule the South but they better not mess with his family in any way. If white hobos—we called them tramps—came up from the railroad seeking a glass of water, he would yell that they were not to enter the gate to his yard. He would have someone take the water out to the road to them. Likewise, if we were working in the field adjacent to the road and white men appeared, he would send someone out to the road to ask their business. White men were never allowed in the field where he and his family were working. I was born into and grew up in his house.

Life was hazardous in Mississippi in the 1940s and 1950s. One had to master a sense of tasks and a sense of place early or pay heavy dues. Poppa was legislator, Supreme Court justice, pope, and king of his house. More than once I saw him administer physical punishment to grown children for talking back to him in his house. I even saw him threaten to kill a white constable, who had come to arrest his son, because he knew white men beat black men after they were arrested. "White folks"—that's what he called the law—"if you touch one strand of hair on my boy I'm gon kill you," he said in a negotiation process which lasted an hour or so and was resolved only when the law allowed him to accompany them and his son to jail.

Patriarchal and demanding, he did not want his wife, Mattie, whom he called Mat, working in the fields. She ran the house, cooked, washed and ironed, and tended to her garden and flower yards as well as the children. His family and their health was his pride and joy. On Saturday he would go to Jackson, where a daughter and a son lived. He would shop a little and eat at Home Dining Room and return home with fables of his trip. Every first and third Sunday morning found him preparing to go to Mount Hood, his church, where he was a deacon and served as treasurer. Momma would accompany him to church sometimes, and I observed early the art of dressing up Grandfather to go out. Every wrinkle had to be set straight and every spot erased. In the rural community I was born into, a man's reputation rested upon the outcome of his family: how his wife dressed, cooked, carried herself, how his children behaved. Poppa's eye made sure his reputation was secure in that community.

When I moved to Jackson, I left Poppa behind in a hole across the street from Pleasant Green Church. However, his laughter, his stare, his attempts at humor, and the cadences of his prayer echo in my being every day. Grandfathers are integral parts of the web of imagination. One way of describing my writing is to say it is my search to find my grandfather within me. It was from his world I embarked when I made the imaginary journey into the discovery of writing. I always could hear his voices somewhere beyond ink and papers, boasting of family and wife. His world was within margins set by the legacy of slavery and the trials of sharecropping. Within that domain, he made his house a fortress of will, and nothing could penetrate it from without or within. He led no marches against segregated housing, sat-in at no lunch counters, and made no freedom rides. He was a black peasant with pride who reared seven children and seven grandchildren on the ungrateful earth of several plantations.

He was a hero because he overcame obstacles and met fate with élan. He is African-American culture and American history. He smelled of dirt and hard work, wore patched overalls, and sometimes used cardboard to cover holes in his shoes. He accepted himself as a child of God. He exhibited his masculinity with pride. I owe my belief that the culture of slaves and their descendants is authentic African culture to my grandfather. Let him laugh and I am behind the mask of Yoruba. Let him curse and Shango breathes lightning. Let him walk and the limbs of a thousand tribes appear.

Grandfathers are that part of your being you fear, you want wrapped behind a dusty photograph somewhere. You display grandmothers; they are the centerpieces of your history. You can put them on mantels or coffee tables. But grandfathers endure, challenge, overcome, succumb to tragedy, yet remain constant—call us to act, stand up, take charge. They are ancestral almanacs detailing possibility for us. In African-American life, grandfathers are mythic figures who lead you across one generation to the next, across one realm of reality to the next, and across galaxies of chaos to some station where courses may yet be charted.

My Grandpa Blondie

Lori Marie Carlson

So many scents.
Sweet pipe smoke and wine-red leather,
worn to cracks from many sittings near the fireplace,
pink peonies in the backyard,
blue-gray Concord grapes,
and sharp cheddar cheese, the kind
that Swedes eat with their freshly baked
cardamom braid, a pomander of paradise,
at Christmastime
the sticky pungency of pine.

My grandpa Blondie
calls to mind a cornucopia of
perfumes from the home.

Memories of dancing, too. At
four, he grabbed my little hand
and did the schottische in the living room,
a kind of summery music in the background,

coming from the old Victrola,
tickling our hearts.

Although he died when I was only five,
I know my grandpa very well. From my own memories,
from those of Grandma (every time she mentioned him she
cried), and from my father's sky-blue eyes that
water
when he takes the family album out and
points to Grandpa working in the rock garden
on Elliot Avenue.

So many years later, living in a city far
from Grandpa's old house, far from Blondie's
values, his community, his culture,
I know that he is with me.
My blond-haired, fair-faced guardian
angel.
A clairvoyant in the town of Lily Dale
told me so. "When you made the jump
from one world to another, a small place
to a city, he was with you, holding
your right hand, allowing you to make the journey
safe and sound."

I believe her.
She clarified the mystery:
why unmistakable, delicious scents of
lovesick flowers, rising dough, and raisin incense
hover, even now,
around me.

Grandfathers: They Speak Through Me

ⓖⓖⓖ

Haki R. Madhubuti

his father's father prepared him to bite his tongue,
power-listening became his gateway to information & race
   knowledge.
his mother's father embraced him fully with large hugs and
words of "can-do" possibilities in a time of darkness and
   treachery.
i was their blood mixture, their bone, their claim to
   immortality & song.

grandfather graves declared white people deficient,
   diseased, & dangerous,
he had scars documenting it, he, an african-black laborer,
   could fix
anything moving that had a motor, a self-taught mechanic
who was gang-beaten at twenty-two for correcting a white
   man at a
chevy dealership at a time when the accepted attitude in

arkansas for
negroes in the presence of whites was head bowed, eyes
    deep to the ground.
quiet. defeated.

grandfather lee, a bronze-colored detroit minister of the
    baptist persuasion,
never worked a day for white folks, god talked to him early
    & he kept his smile.
he pastored to a community where eyes & work seldom said
    no or "can't do," starting
from a storefront, growing into a used movie theater, to
    building from the earth
up, into a fifteen-hundred-seat stained-glass, concrete, and
    fine-wood cathedral, this became
an answer. god was his mission, his people, his melody, &
    neither *quit* nor *quiet* was
in him. he anchored bronzeville, negotiated with white
    stones, had what his
congregation called good backup, the solid feed of osun,
    obatala, and shango.

at six i was at their knees consuming words, jerks, silences,
    and secrets.
at eleven i was taken to the woods & left with knife, water,
    and a map, manhood
was coming. soon.

at thirteen i was taken to the pulpit, given the bible,
  songbook, and silver watch,
jesus was in the air & always on time.
at fourteen i discovered richard wright, louis armstrong,
  chester himes, miles davis,
langston hughes, gwendolyn brooks, and motown. i was
  branded crazy, insolent, &
world-wounded for the questions i asked & for the burn in
  my eyes.
as a young man i carried many knowledges, ran between
  two cultures,
cleared my head in the military & libraries & cried for the
  loss of my mother.
i kissed girls and black politics on the g.i. bill in college
  and was exiled
into black struggle in the early sixties. i learned to ride the
  winds of battle.

as a man i choose poetry, love, & extended family,
i selected black independence, institution building, &
the cheery eyes of children as my mission.
i breathe the smoke & oxygen from the fires of my
  grandfathers,
i have their slow smile, quick mind, and necessary wit,
i wear their earth shoes & dance with their languages,
i speak in the cadences of southern trees, holy water, &
  books,
i carry their messages & courageous hearts,

my eyes are ancestor deep, bold, & intrepid,
i whisper their songs as mantras,
my music is accelerated blues, the four tops and trane.
it is they, my grandfathers, who taught me the notes &
    rhythms
and as the son of their sons
i'm not missing a beat.

grandfather poem

(for Albert B. Cleage, Sr., and Merschell C. Graham)

Pearl Cleage

fathers are often
new to the gig
awkward
filled with expectations
needs   egos   longing
wondering when things
are going to get back
to normal

by the time
granddaddies
come on the scene
they have already
survived it
moved on to once
removed vigilant
but once removed

affectionate but uninvolved
eyes fixed on a point
a little above our heads
a little to the right
of our dreams & visions
filled with expectations
needs   egos   longing
but once removed

we are their children
sure as sunrise
we are their loving legacy
defiantly imperfect, trembling
on the edge of immortality

watching you
teach us how

John Allen Kirkland

Minister, Teacher, Father, Pastor, Confidant,
a Credible Image, and the Shaper of a Grandson
(1868–1942)

Walter J. Leonard

I was nearly eight years old when members of our family finally accepted a very painful truth: Papa, as my grandfather was affectionately known, had lost his sight. Those eyes which had flashed so warmly, which had seen so much, had guided so many people, had read so many books, had taught so many pupils, had helped to preach so many sermons, and, above all, had shown the mysteries and joys of reading and learning to a grandson, would not see the faces of his children or behold the beauty of nature again.

I was devastated. My grandfather would not be able to point to birds, trees, buildings, books, paintings, cartoons, and people, and, in his uniquely instructive way help me to see differences and/or similarities in God's creations and man's creativity.

He had given me my first primer/primary reader and my first Bible and my first dictionary. I could recall his explanation of the dictionary and its importance: "Jay, son, this book will help you to understand all of the other books; it tells you what every word means; it is like a key to a place where you have never been; it will open the door and show you what is there; you should read and study the dictionary just as you would any other book."

But, as disheartening, and as injuring, as the news of his blindness had been, I was soon to realize that our lives were to become even more interwoven. For the remaining years of his life, eight years, I would become his *seeing-eye*. He would take my arm, usually the right one, and we would travel from place to place; short or long, the distance and the destination did not matter; we were comfortable with each other, grandfather and grandson, spanning three generations together.

During those remaining years, Papa used my mind as a tape recorder. The variety of subjects and the words of wisdom were often beyond the immediate attention or intellectual grasp of one at such a tender age. But so very much was remembered, assimilated, appreciated, and applied.

"Son, in life, it is important to set your goals high, wide, and long. You must then go as far as you can see; but don't stop there. Once you reach that point, it is from there that you must see just how much farther you can go."

There were times when I would tell him about my disappointment in the conduct of a friend or an acquaintance, and my grandfather would remind me that the test of friendship is sometimes difficult for some people to pass. "Jay, try to always remember that a true friend is one who shows up at the showdown; many times that is too much to expect of a lukewarm friendship."

We took several bus rides. Two, in particular, stand out: a bus ride from Savannah, Georgia (our home), to Atlanta, Georgia, because he wanted me to see Morehouse College and the Atlanta University complex of colleges and seminaries; and from Atlanta we traveled by bus to Nashville, Tennessee, because he wanted me to see Jubilee Hall and Fisk University. I saw those important institutional landmarks through the eyes of a blind man.

Another trip took us from Savannah to Hawkinsville, Georgia, where, for the last time, I would see and visit with my maternal great-grandfather Isaac Shivers (aka Isaac Showers). I was always thrilled, surprised, saddened, and a bit angry when he would tell about the "bad and sad days of slavery, days when you didn't own yourself"; and about the times when he had been beaten, "for no good reason," just to be reminded that he was property, not considered a person, but a slave, an African in America; and that he dare not demonstrate any capacity to learn, think, or have an opinion. Complete denial of self was expected and demanded by slaveholders. When he died in 1942, he was nearly a hundred years old.

Back to my grandfather. There are and were so many witticisms, and words of wisdom and advice, that I first heard from him. I will share just a few:

"Son, you can do your best learning when someone else is talking; when you are paying attention, listening."

"Jay, when you want people to help you, you have to win them over, and you must remember it is much like fishing: if you want the fish to bite, you have to fish with what the fish like, not with what you like."

"Given the way our people have been treated in this country, don't forget that your very presence, your ability to survive, with dignity, is in itself a very real victory."

"Be careful when you are talking to new people, strangers.
If you talk with five people five minutes and they don't
know anyone that you know, then move on, for you are talking to the wrong people; you are likely to be in the wrong
company."

"Not all white people are bad, even when it seems that
way. And not all colored people are good. There are white
people who will help you, and there are colored people who
will stand in your way. Just remember, you have to be better than white people to get their respect, and you have to
show colored people that you wish them well."

"Jay, son, remember, there is no such person or thing as
Tarzan. That is another white-man's lie!"

" 'Amos and Andy' and 'Beulah' are mean and derogatory;
they are dumb and retarded; they are not true. Those things
have nothing to do with you."

"Save your money and watch your conduct. You never
want to live longer than your good name, and you don't
want to outlive your money. God will always help you if you
help yourself."

"Son, don't let anyone tell you that white people are
smarter. White children might have better books, bigger
schools, and more money. But God knew we would have to
suffer in order to save His world, so He gave you a better
brain, better manners, and a better family. Nobody is better
than you!"

In the years when we talked, walked, and traveled together, I would read articles, newspapers, and books for his information and reaction. I remember his observation about Franklin Delano Roosevelt: "Mr. Roosevelt is a good man. But we colored people [he did not like the term "Negro"] have had only one president; that was Abraham Lincoln. He was the only one that ever kept his promise to us. Maybe we will have another one like him. So far, Andrew Johnson and Woodrow Wilson were the worst, and Abraham Lincoln was the best. You must read about and study all of the presidents. We sure do need another Lincoln."

"W.J., there is no substitute for education. Everybody needs to know a lot just to get up in the morning. And as an African in America you will need to know more than white people. Knowledge is the foundation of a good life, of a good job, and the wealth that you will need for your family. Nobody can take knowledge from you. Some may not like you because you know things. But even the ones who may not like you will have to respect you."

"The key things to remember when you have a job: always be punctual, be polite, work hard, learn all that you can about the job and everything connected with it, respect your employer and make sure he respects you, make sure you are properly dressed, and don't forget—as long as someone else signs your paycheck you are always looking for another job."

John Allen Kirkland was born in the midst of the malevolence of the American South, in 1868, shortly after America's official Holocaust, chattel slavery, had been declared illegal and over. But he lived, survived the continuing evil of segregation, the meanness of daily bias, the ugly specter of lynchings, the awful hypocrisy of the nation's political, civic, and religious leaders. He became a preacher, "Minister of the Gospel," as he would put it; a student of the Scriptures and a teacher who attracted young and old to the joy and utility of reading and learning. He could hold audiences spellbound as his voice would rise and fall—with a well-timed pause. He always demonstrated a caring for others and a reverence for life—characteristics that were contagious. He always felt that he had been called upon to help in diminishing the suffering and pain of others.

To me, he was the embodiment of the oft-heard statement "the salt of the earth." It was my opinion that God made a few like Papa, and sprinkled people like him around to keep the world from spoiling, to keep men's actions from smelling too bad.

By 1942, the time of his death, the United States had fought several wars, and two of John Allen Kirkland's four sons and one of his five daughters were in the uniform of the United States military. I, his grandson, would join them in 1945.

After seventeen months in the military, I returned to civilian life; and, as my grandfather had instructed and predicted, I set out to follow his advice: Get an education! Recently, I was appointed as a visiting scholar at Wolfson College, Oxford University, Oxford, England. Papa's spirit is somewhere, comfortable in the knowledge that his efforts toward shaping my life were not in vain.

Grandpa: Appendage to HIS/sTORY

(for Thomas Smallwood)

Joanne V. Gabbin

1.

The arm kept me from knowing you.
It smelled bad like the dead mouse
Lying just under the backyard steps.
I was glad you kept it covered.
I turned my head when Mama bathed you,
But once I saw that it was dark and flaky
Like a shedding snake's skin.
It did not look like the rest of you.

Every evening, Mama called me to take your dinner.
Just when the *Buddy Dean Show* came on
And I'm set to laugh at the white kids trying to dance,
She would say, "Take this to Pa and be careful."
I'd run across Broadway, up the stairs
To your room, to that smell.

One day I came and your arm was gone.
I saw the flattened space under your sleeve.

THOMAS SMALLWOOD

My words came fast as I handed you the plate
Wrapped in a torn brown paper bag:

"Grandpa, here's your supper.
  I'll pick up the plate tomorrow."

And then I ran down the stairs,
Out the door, across the boulevard,
Up the white marble steps,
Warped from constant scrubbing,
To the safeness of my house
Where there was no smell of death.

Mama told me later how you lost your arm,
How your hand went dead and gangrene set in,
About the delay with the consent papers,
And how you almost died.
Mama told me a lot of stories about you
When I was ready to know and remember.

2.

Mama said there was a time your arms steadied the plow
When the mule lurched wildly off-course.
Through seasons of cotton, corn, and soybeans,
You planted in the sandy North Carolina soil,
Through Depression harvests that barely fed
The hunger of your soul.

Your children grew too,
Eleven head of them

Pushing their way into the world
On the prayers of a wife you called "Sister."
Tom, Jay, Biggie,
Peenane, Rayfield, Georgia, Bus,
Jessie, Ugabe, Nellie, and Mae Alice,
Too many to take with you in the Ford jalopy
Bought with years of putting back dreams,
Too many for the ten-dollar room on Eager Street
That would be your waiting place.

3.

Mama said there was a time you knelt on the wailing floor.
Your six-foot-two-inch frame
Accordioned in submission,
Your broad shoulders bending
Like a tuning fork over treasure.
You prayed like you sat with the Shepherd,
Prayed like your petitions went straight to Glory:

  "Lord, here I am on bended knee
   Asking that you bless this woman
   Done toiled with me these many years,
   Raised our chillen to fear you,
   Done pressed her way in your service. . . ."

Then you stopped talking to God in public
And left the altar, too soon shrouded in her memory.

4.

Mama said there was a time you were loud enough
To drown out your loneliness.

The city was ripe like the watermelons
You loaded on the horse-drawn wagon.
Ripe as one you plugged
To show off the redness at the heart.
"Arabing" through the Baltimore streets,
You called out, more of a cantor than a seller,

  "Watermelon—Watermelon
   Red to the rind
   Get your ripe, red Watermelonnnn"

And folks would come out of their oppressive row houses
Wanting a nickel slice or a dime piece to carry back.
It would cool their tongues and sweeten their lot.

5.

Mama reminded me that you ran a store on Gay Street,
Before urban renewal took away its spirit.
I remember the rounds of cheddar cheese
Wrapped in gauze stiff with wax,
Pickled pigfeet pressed against the glass jars,
Codfish cakes covered sparingly with waxed paper,
Only a pretense against the swarming flies,
And beef jerky you kept for the special customers
Waiting for their ride to the furnaces of Bethlehem Steel.
And we grandkids came to eye the Mary Janes and the
Southies,
Tasting the syrupy sweet in our minds before we
unwrapped them:

"Grandpa, Grandpa, can I have two?
    Mama lets me have candy before dinner."

Before the city planners blocked off Gay Street
And made it a plaza that nobody used,
There were sounds of prosperity in your store.

6.

The arm kept me from knowing you then.
Now it is an appendage to your story.
It draws me out of the safeness of my house,
Across the boulevard, up the steps
Of the three-story row house
To your room where you wait for your supper.

Then I see a chair beside your bed.
I am surprised to remember it was always there.

Grand Daddy Warren

Chester Higgins, Jr.

The Reverend Warren Smith, a stout man of average height, balding, and clean-shaven with hair growing out of his ears, was my grandfather. He was an accomplished tailor, owner of our New Brockton, Alabama, dry cleaners as well as the minister of three churches. A ready smile matched his cheerful disposition. Everyone loved him and he them.

Up until his death when I was thirteen, my grandfather's guiding hand helped chisel the milestones of my life. It was my grandfather who witnessed, and interpreted, the vision that snatched my sleep at the age of nine. I awoke to a blinding, vibrating brightness. Within the light appeared the figure of a man. He walked toward me with outstretched hands, palms up. And then he said, "I want you." In that instant, terror took hold and my own screaming voice filled my ears. All the adults in the house—my grandparents and parents—burst into my room. After they had calmed me a bit, I was able to tell them what I had seen and how the air rattled with energy around the being.

The Reverend Warren Smith

Everyone, except my grandfather, the Reverend Warren Smith, was baffled. He was certain I had just had a vision calling me to the ministry. I preached from the pulpit in Alabama for over a decade, and to this day I follow the spirit.

My grandfather gave me my first driving lesson when I was just eight years old. He did this even after I had forced his car off the road during a hard rain a year or so earlier. I was sitting next to him in the front passenger seat when the car skidded on a patch of mud. We were sliding downhill all across the road. Watching him fight with the steering wheel, I thought my grandfather must be having a heart attack, so I grabbed the steering wheel to straighten us out. Abruptly the car left the road, and we landed in the ditch. No one was hurt, and after the initial shock my grandfather was more amused than angry.

My grandfather also taught me how to knot a suit tie. I stood in front of the mirror working the tie as he sat at his sewing machine making clothes in his dry-cleaning shop and my father worked the presser. After watching numerous tie-tying failures, my grandfather stood up. "Let me help you," was all he said. He explained the knotting sequence, straightening the tie back out and guiding my hands on the fabric. And then he let me do it by myself. I remember touching the precious knot before trying to retrace the steps he had just shown me. I looked in the mirror and then at him for reassurance and, when necessary, direction. It took a few tries, but I got it. Thrilled, I strutted around the shop displaying this knot of my own making. My grandfather gave me his congratulations, laughing with pleasure. Then he went back to his work.

It wasn't until I became an adult that I began to discover that this gentle man, whose strength was always there for me, was a staunch pioneer for the improvement of the lives of all African-American people. He had withstood racial slurs, threats, and even having his house burned down for his struggles to secure voting and schooling for African Americans in Coffee County. Before 1928, powerful landowners allowed only white kids to be educated in the county. The Reverend Warren Smith petitioned the County Board of Education to pay teachers' salaries if he provided the land and the building for a school. He converted the Masonic Lodge to accommodate five classes on two floors, and the nearby Collins Chapel AME Church served the over-flow. He headed the search committee that found the first teacher, Mr. Paul Anthony Youngblood. Later, when the county school board offered an old vacant school building in another part of the county, my grandfather with help from other school trustees organized the community to salvage lumber and restraighten nails from this derelict school building. Two carpenters, Mr. Milton Yelverton and Mr. Les Flowers, were hired to organize and instruct all the volunteers. This band of dedicated citizens built our first school building on land owned by my grandfather.

Voting in rural Alabama in the 1930s was a rich man's sport. To vote you had to own property or, failing that, pay a poll tax each and every time you voted. My grandfather, a landowner, was not affected by these insidious Jim Crow laws, but he never forgot those without land. He and other African-American landowners brought folks by the carload to the polls and paid the tax so they could be heard.

My grandfather touched all who dealt with him. His genuine and positive spirit proved to be a powerful and inspirational catalyst for change. Today I stand upon his broad shoulders, secure in his guidance and love.

WAS TOO TALL FOR THE SHELF

Four Words

Marina Budhos

I never met my grandfather, which is exactly how he wanted it.

The day my mother told her parents that she was going to marry a dark, handsome Indian man from the Caribbean, my Jewish grandfather retreated into his bedroom, sat down on the bed, and said four words in Yiddish: "You have shamed us." From that day on, he refused to have anything to do with his only daughter, never met his son-in-law, and never set eyes on his two grandchildren.

My grandparents were Orthodox Jews from Russia, first cousins whose marriage was arranged shortly after they each settled in Brooklyn, New York. They lived next door to the synagogue, ran a grocery together, and reared their daughter, expecting order and obedience in their home. During my mother's exile, my grandmother kept up a secret life—visiting us in our small apartment in Jackson Heights, Queens, writing fretful letters to my mother when she stayed for months with my father's family in Guyana.

ISIDORE ZALTZMAN

Eight years after she married, my mother received a desperate call from her mother: my grandfather was in the hospital. At the time, my brother was seven, and I had just turned one. Upon arriving at the hospital, my mother was told by the doctors that my grandfather had, at most, six weeks to live. She and my grandmother chose not to tell him the truth of his condition. So she headed into that hospital room, heavy with the knowledge of her father's death, aware that this was her final goodbye and yet, strangely enough, her first hello since she had begun her new life. Propped up in his bed, my grandfather greeted her with a characteristically half-critical, half-approving remark: "So, I hear your floors are so clean you can eat off of them!"

She laughed. This was the language between parent and child that she knew so well—love and duty, entwined like two barbed wires, each piercing the other.

My grandfather died the day before Yom Kippur, the holiest day of the year, when Jews fast and pray, ask for forgiveness, and atone for their sins. By Jewish law, a person must be buried immediately after death in a plain wooden coffin wrapped in a prayer shawl. Since this was a High Holiday, my mother and grandmother could not find a rabbi, and had to bury my grandfather the day after. My mother took care of all the arrangements, listening, at the burial, to the gossip around her from family friends and relatives, the murmurs from people who had thought she was dead. Somehow, she had made her peace with her father; somehow, on that rainy, difficult Yom Kippur in 1961, she found her way to forgiveness.

I'm not sure I ever did.

Years later, when I was writing my first novel, which was partially based on my mother's early break with her family, I tried to imagine this man, who so coldly turned his back on his only daughter; who lived only a subway ride away from us, but chose not to see his own grandchildren.

I was spending a month at Yaddo, a writer's colony, and worked in a round tower room where I spread old photographs in a circle on the windowsill. I also read letters my mother had written during her time in Guyana. They were mostly reassurances to a worried mother, though underneath I could read my grandmother's sense of abandonment. In all these letters, my grandfather was oddly out of the picture. Did he hear about his chubby grandson, spoiled by his Caribbean-Indian aunts? Or his skinny daughter, gaining weight and nurtured back to health, as she was fed on mangoes and coconut milk and chicken curry?

In that bright and sunny room, my grandfather stared back at me, bald and bland, hardly the image of a fearsome, tyrannical Jewish patriarch. The photo showed him behind the counter at a grocery, a place he worked after his own business failed. He was apple-cheeked, yet melancholy, inward-looking. He was forcing the smile. He looked out of place next to the signs for eggs and cheese, the weighing scale. He wore his white grocer's coat like a costume. My grandfather hated being a grocer. If it weren't for the pogroms in Russia that drove my family from Uman, just outside Kiev, he would have remained at his yeshiva, studying in his airy citadel of words, retreating from the world of flesh-and-blood loyalties and conflicts.

Maybe we weren't so different, I thought, as I scribbled away in my own writer's tower. I understood the power of words—how they harm; how they show love; how they are also an act of faith.

My grandfather was happiest reading the Talmud, or listening to the soulful swell and rise of opera on his 78 records. America, with all its swift changeability, terrified him. There is a story that one day, soon after he arrived in the country, his younger brother came driving up in a car and invited him for a ride. My grandfather got in the passenger seat, but was so frightened he stepped out while the car was still moving. That was my grandfather: stubbornly braced against the modern world, even as events propelled him forward.

My grandfather was a cohen, one of the priest class who perform particular rituals during the synagogue ceremonies. During the Depression, when he was forced to keep his store open on the Sabbath, he turned his back on the synagogue, and never went again. If he could not observe completely, he would not observe at all. In the same way, if his daughter would not obey him, then she was no daughter at all.

This starkness, this cold extremism, became his legacy. For I knew my grandfather through my mother's own rages when she felt wronged, and disagreement was seen as disobedience. I learned that authority could not be questioned. God demanded that Abraham sacrifice his son Isaac to prove his devotion. Duty and obedience were all.

Still, there was a difference in my life. My mother inherited the language of stormy rejection, but she had also suffered through her father's barbed silence. She would never fully turn her back on me, as her own father had done. Her anger was also an expression of pained attachment.

That Jewish knot of pain and rejection remained inside me. I married a Jewish man, under a huppah, and my grandfather would be shocked to know that he is, ironically, a cohen, the grandson of the chief rabbi of Kiev. He is also a man who lives by the word, as an editor and a scholar, and who loves nothing better than to listen to opera. And in me, too, there is still a small, querulous, Old Testament core, a right-from-wrong ethical-mindedness that runs strong and deep. I am drawn to the mysterious beauty and purity of ritual, but I can never forgive a man who, like Abraham, loved his God, his tradition, more than his own flesh and blood.

There is a Jewish proverb: "A blow passes, but a word remains." With those four words—"You have shamed us"— my grandfather may have turned his back on us, but his words remained. His was a powerful silence, reaching across generations, damaging and shaping, teaching us a fierce, uncompromising language of pain and exile. And like it or not, my grandfather lived on with us, no matter how hard he tried to stay away.

The Point of No Return

Jonathan Patton

There is a rumor going around
the small Texas town of Hereford,
where I was born.
Hushed whispers are saying
that the admired and respected Dr. Richard Patton
is having a tryst with the attractive, young,
and newly widowed Mary Lou Martin.
This is causing quite an uproar in the Patton clan
and I, the favorite grandson,
was instructed to confront Grandpa Dick.

The next Sunday, after church,
Grandpa looked at me with his old
Pekinese-like face set in a blank stare,
his yellow nails tapping lightly
on the side of his favorite
"Everyone Loves Dick" coffee mug,
as I explained the family's concern.

He smiled slightly, showing a sliver of
off-white dentures, and explained
in an almost mockingly serious tone
about the Point of No Return.

He said in his low gravelly voice,
"Well, Johnny-boy,
you're a man now and I suppose you should know
that there comes a day
when you will awaken and turn
to your wife of four or five decades and realize—
and know
that you will never
hold her like you used to.
You'll look lovingly at her aged wrinkled face
and not be able to make yourself
kiss her dry thin lips.
You'll examine her sun-marked cheeks
and imagine that if you listen very closely
you can hear the sound of her jowls falling.
You'll think of her sagging bosom
and fallen bottom that weigh
like sacks of russet potatoes
hung from her body
and know they will never excite you again.
On that morning you will hope
that you can still love this woman
that you will never lust for again.
And I do love your grandmother very much

and would never leave her unprovided for.
I wish it didn't hurt her, but
a man can't just stop living."

I nodded and
understood that his words were true.
The family was ecstatic to be assured
that Grandpa Dick was guilty
of no impropriety
and would never
invite another woman
into his bed.

Good and Bad

Liz Rosenberg

My grandfather was a lot of bad things:
a butcher,
a gambler,
and mostly very poor.
He told me on the long boatride over
from Russia to America he had to eat hay,
and it tasted good,
he said, like chop suey.
One time we played baseball
in the dim little knickknack apartment on Flatbush.
My home run brought the mantelpiece down,
Grandma's china figurines and all.
He grabbed my hand and said,
"Come on! We better get OUTA here."
So we ran and hid in the Brooklyn Museum,
where I counted the rings on a slice of tree.
That tree was older than even my grandpa.
My other grandfather was good and rich.

He had a bird whistle he wouldn't share
in his backyard at Palm Beach, Florida.
My poor grandpa always came visiting
with a wrinkled paper bag of Almond Kisses in his hand,
and a smile on his wicked face.

From Mining the Family Branches

Matt Lichtel

Recalling when we were young
Is not so easy without a table of contents.

I've been away too long to know
What once-removed coal dust tastes like.

How does a man give his life and manage to live it?
Is a rock hammer valued more if made of gold?

He made us what we are and knows what is to become of us.
He gave us what we have and we can only hope to hand it
    back.

Preparing coal to become diamond
Can land a person upon my page.

Mining facts without truth
Make poets cringe at glitter and gleam.

What can we do to give thanks to soul creators?
How much different is a spade from a club, a diamond from
  a heart?

He is a glittering diamond that shines while I live.
He knew the railroad, coal mines, time, and love so that we
  may know happiness.

The Story Goes

Lydie Raschka

The story goes that my handsome Norwegian grandfather, Ole Olson, left the farm where he was raised in northern Michigan to go to Detroit, where he found a job as a dishwasher at the hospital. He met a pretty nurse named Dorothy, fell in love, and had two children: the first, my aunt Greta, born deaf; the second, my dad, Nels. There are intimations (there are always intimations): Dorothy married beneath her and was mentally unstable, Ole was a womanizer, she didn't want children. But this is a family that doesn't relish telling stories, so much is not clear; I'll move on to the facts instead. They divorced, Dorothy wanted to be an actress, she drove to Hollywood with a man, she killed herself in a car high on a hill above the city, making front-page news with the headline "Starstruck." Nels was five and Greta was seven when their mother died.

It's a lot of drama for a man who doesn't talk much. I never once heard him speak about any of it. It can be maddening—a quiet person, what was he thinking? I inherited

OLE OLSON

it. Every year my report card from elementary school said, *Needs to learn to speak up in a group.* I've had to learn to speak: living in New York, speak or never get your bagel.

After their mother left for Hollywood, Nels and Greta lived with Dorothy's parents until Ole could earn enough money to get a house. When Nels was a second-grader he went back to live with his dad. "Were you happy to be back with him?" I asked, trying to get my mind around my dad at seven living without a parent. "Yes, I guess I was," he said as though it had never occurred to him before—the happiness or sadness of it. It's the way Grandpa was; he accepted his life without comment but he was grateful for the good that came his way.

When we were little he bought frilly pastel dresses for my sisters and me—Christmas, Easter, birthdays. But the shopping got too complicated as we grew older and the dresses stopped coming. Then it was a card bought by my mother and signed "Love, Grandpa Ole." In college I wrote him letters, when reminded by my parents, but letters weren't very important to him. I have never seen him write anything more than "Love, Grandpa Ole," except maybe once he wrote, "Miss you." He communicated his love for us, his complete acceptance of us, the fact that he thought we were beautiful, through silence.

A friend once said to me, "You are the quietest person I ever met." A dubious distinction. People read into silence, and so they read my grandpa the way they wanted to: Was he dumb? Was he depressed? *Could* he talk? He left the farm to seek a more interesting life and ended up raising two children alone.

More than he bargained for, but something he took on and achieved with an admirable steadiness and few words.

He lived in a nursing home the last two years of his life. When my dad went to visit he could see that women were still attracted to his father—so tall and gentle and calm at ninety. Women wanted to mother him, feed him, fuss over him. He had big creases beside his mouth which on a happier person might be called smile lines. My dad pulled Ole's cheek back to smooth out the lines for shaving. He does the same with his own face now.

At his wife's funeral someone spied Ole sitting in his car outside the church. He never went in. I think I can understand that; his emotions were not for others to witness. If he was asked about the past he shook his head, said, "I don't remember." When we went to spend time with him on the farm where he was raised he opened up the way quiet people often do when they are in comfortable surroundings with people they love. He cooked big breakfasts with bacon and eggs and potatoes. He had projects: fix the tractor, take the grandchildren for a ride in the trailer, repair the roof. He liked deer hunting with the other men, but no one can remember him ever killing a deer.

The rest of his life was without drama. He lived to be ninety-two, exercising every morning. He had girlfriends but never remarried. He lived an hour away from us. He sat in a chair at our house nodding off to sleep while we fought and wrestled and grew up around him. He finally sold the farm, then got it back, then sold it again. Afterward he said, "I never should have sold that farm."

Grandpa only said a few words to me: "You eat like a bird." Turning to my dad, he'd say it again, "She eats like a bird." Actually, I'm tall and a hearty eater. But I was picky: no raisins or nuts in anything, no shellfish, no fat on the meat. Now I'm almost a vegetarian; then I was just picky. What Grandpa saw was discipline, a girl who watched her figure as he watched his. It was his way of saying, "You have the ability to do anything you want to do." I can't remember anything else he said, but it doesn't matter. Talking was not his strong point.

I called his apartment just minutes after he died. I knew he was sick and I felt a need to talk to him. It was a little difficult finding the number; I had never called. The nurse was confused by the timing of the call—not sure—did I know he was dead? She realized I couldn't know, it had just happened, so she didn't tell me the news; instead she passed the phone to my dad, who was visiting his father when he died. It's always been that way for me. The silent connection is the strongest one of all.

Nana

᠖᠖᠖

Sanjay Nigam

Just before he died at the age of eighty-five, my grandfather began to remind me of Yoda, the Jedi Master of the *Star Wars* trilogy. Not only did he look a little like Yoda, he seemed to have something of Yoda's crankiness, not to mention his wisdom. Throughout my late teens—roughly around the time the *Star Wars* movies came out—my grandfather Nana was as close to a guide as I ever had. Even now, in my own middle years, Nana—who saw *The Sound of Music* seven times, corresponded with Mother Teresa, acted as an adviser to a world-famous maharishi, and in his final years became a member of a euthanasia society—remains one of the most interesting people I've known.

They say a grandparent's love, unlike a parent's, is unselfish. There's something to this, for I feel that Nanima, my grandmother, Nana's wife, loves me in exactly this way—wholly, unselfishly. With Nana it was different. I was the son he never really had, and his expectations were those of a father. I think he was a little confused about his role as well,

and there were many times I couldn't figure out what he
wanted. Nobody else's grandfather seemed as concerned over
which roads he was taking in life. Sometimes I wished Nana
would just offer grandfatherly affection and nothing else.
But that wouldn't have been easy for Nana, and even if it
was, he couldn't be that way with me.

For a long time, I thought Nana was a great man, sort of
like Jawaharlal Nehru, India's first prime minister, whom he
very much admired. There were some parallels. Like Nehru,
Nana was a handsome man, broadly educated, proud, and
headstrong. He spoke and wrote literary English. Nana was
jailed for participating in the Quit India movement against
the British. After the Brits left, he was one of the first officers of the Indian Administrative Service, the corps of civil-
service officers that, under Nehru, ran newly independent
India. It was a big deal, then, for these men essentially re-
placed the British government, and for many years were
treated like royalty and wielded the power of minor princes.
And, like an Indian prince, Nana once shot a tiger.

Nana was an insomniac, and since I too was a bad sleeper,
whenever I visited him in New Delhi we often found ourselves lying around grumpily in the living room at three
o'clock in the hot summer night, waiting for dawn to break
and the old housekeeper to bring morning tea. By seven
o'clock, as many as three newspapers would have been delivered, and we'd keep drinking tea, swapping pages without a
word until we were completely saturated with the news.
And then we'd begin to talk. Our discussions could go any-
where. The topics were strange, and sometimes my replies

didn't seem particularly grandsonlike, nor were his grandfatherlike, and the awkwardness would make us both irritated and argumentative. At other times, we were off into vaguely philosophical realms; he loved to compare East and West. We'd take breaks, do our own things, and then continue our discussion in the late afternoon or evening—or talk about something new. History, reminiscences about his early days in the civil service, whatever. And so it would go—until bedtime, and then start again in the morning. I'm amazed that I still remember some of it, sad that I've forgotten so much.

As optimism about the Indian experiment waned—as the results began to seem ambiguous at best—Nana became more pessimistic and then a little ambivalent. By that time, Nana was nearing retirement. I'd entered my mid-teens, and that was when I really began to know him. As the years went by, I began to see Nana's many limitations, occasionally pointing them out to him, though now I realize that he had perceived them long before. And when I think back on the hundreds of letters he wrote me—some of them loving though uninteresting, others taunting and unsettling—I realize that he wanted me to do what he could never quite do: hurdle past the mostly internal obstacles that kept tripping him up. He kept telling me I was like Hamlet, someone with noble ideals, and even a little wherewithal to achieve some of them, if it wasn't for my indecisiveness, my tendency to wallow in anxieties. I rolled my eyes while he recited lines from Shakespeare, especially *Hamlet.* That was him, I said, not me. He was seeing himself in me, poor old man.

Perhaps it's just genetics, but Nana turned out to be right. Comparing me to Hamlet just dignifies a certain weakness of spirit that I will battle throughout my life. Only now do I have a clue about Nana's frustrations with himself, his sense of falling much shorter than he ever should have. I still believe he was made from a heroic mold, but there were some cracks where it counted. And as I grapple with my own frustrations in life, I sometimes wonder if I'm just going to repeat the mistakes of my grandfather. Although the setting and cast are different, is it only a variation of the same old story? I hope not, but I fear so. And yet I take a little, perhaps perverse, comfort in knowing that my story is similar to Nana's.

The last time I cried was the night I heard Nana died. He'd dozed off while watching TV and fell over, breaking his hipbone. He underwent surgery at the hospital, but there was one stupid complication after another. I wanted to go to India to help him—as a doctor and the closest thing he had to a son—but I couldn't go, because here in Boston my wife was expecting our firstborn any day, and there was concern that it might be a difficult delivery. My son arrived late, and for a long time I felt guilty. Maybe I could have gone—done my best for Nana as a doctor—and flown back before my son was born. I guess I also felt guilty because I probably should have lit his funeral pyre.

Nana was India for me. Even though I'd grown up in America, as long as Nana was alive I'd felt that I could always choose between India and America—and this was an endless issue of discussion and sometimes tension with

Nana; he badgered me about my being a fake Indian, which was the surest way to rankle me when I was visiting India. Thinking I had a choice between West and East—that it was entirely up to me—somehow made it easier to be a chocolate kid in a world that was mainly vanilla, pretty much the way things were in the Arizona public schools I attended from the late sixties to the mid-seventies. I could always tell myself, If not here, then there. But when Nana died, that other potential life I'd built up in my mind came to an abrupt end. I began to see India as the ancestral land, not necessarily my land.

But the world is, as they say, a strange place. My wife was in labor for twenty-six hours. My son got stuck in the birth canal and had to be pulled out with forceps. His face was slightly squished, though, being a doctor, I knew it would eventually look the way it was meant to. Even so, he looked kind of funny; frankly, it bothered me a bit during those very first minutes of his life. But as I stared at my son, the features on his face began to grow on me—to feel absolutely right. For Kabir, my baby boy, looked like Yoda.

Of Usefulness and Miracles

Karla Farmer Stouse

I had a grandpa of the most useful sort, complete with thick lamb-white hair, smooth green cotton workclothes, and the busy kinds of jobs that fascinate the young and provide the world with its necessities. Since such labors usually follow the dictates of daylight, a timepiece is rarely required; Grandpa's silver railroad watch, old before he was a boy, usually sat on the gunrack shelf. He chose instead to accessorize with a butcher's bloodied apron, a janitor's weighty key-keeper, or a farmer's crusted boots. A genuinely useful man, especially to the five-year-old for whom he invented a miracle—the cherry tomato.

Perhaps you're thinking that the cherry tomato (Grandpa called it a 'mater) was actually invented by Such-and-Such Seed Company before the turn of the century. Of course not. Grandpa said he made those little yellow and red jewels, those orbs that smelled of summer, just for me, just my size, perfect for a five-year-old to pluck and carry three in a hand and pop into her mouth whole, with hardly any juice to escape and leave its trail. And he put plants close to the garden front, so a toad-fearing child wouldn't have to brave the dank wilds of cornstalks and sunflowers and regular tomato plants to harvest them. Would such a man, whose name was really truly John Smith, lie?

Not to his intent little shadow. He never seemed too busy, the way other adults did, to sort through my myriad questions of why people eat beef tongue or how the high-school boiler all the way down in the basement could heat three stories of building or whether horses really prefer to live on the other side of their fences. I never felt like a child—in the negative sense of that word—with him, a man who delighted in teaching me to hook my thumbs in nonexistent belt loops and spit, a man who proudly presented me with a large and expensively beautiful German-shepherd toy he surely couldn't afford, because he knew I hated the white blouses my grandma gave me each Christmas and because he knew I loved animals more than most anything else.

Perhaps he treated me as he did because he found me unlike other children—such as some of my frilly cousins, who feared the barn lot and never stopped at the grocery store or the high school to see what adventures he was creating. They didn't care to know how he made souse or where he fetched sorghum. They didn't feed cows and didn't want to discuss a particular palomino's conformation. They didn't understand the mysteries of putting a seed in the ground and didn't want dirty hands. They wanted dolls to dress instead of trees to climb. Not really very useful to a man whose life was hard work out of the necessity to provide for his family and numerous friends, out of the sheer joy of self-reliance in such honorable pursuits.

I used to think Grandpa's old Chevys were embarrassing eyesores; I have since learned he was a dirt-track racer who knew the craftsmanship of those peeling/rusted hulks, and now that my appreciation has matured, I wouldn't mind one of my own. I used to question the lack of reading materials in his house, knowing that reading was something required of smart people; I have since grasped the concept that pages cannot capture all the world's truths. I used to wonder why he resisted church to risk the clucking condemnations of my grandma and her friends; I have since understood that he knew more of God than most pew-sitters do, and I have felt the rumblings of my own questions about hypocrisy grow louder each year. And I especially used to struggle with his belief that the best garden requires weeding out some perfectly good crops to make room for an abundance of harvest; I have since seen the usefulness of that philosophy time and again. What I couldn't see at five has crystallized at nearly forty: miracles, even small ones like cherry 'maters, need room to grow.

I'm Missing You

Chevis Mitchell (age 16)

You left my life in a painful way,
my heart remains broken until this day.
I miss your laughs, I miss your love;
I shed so many tears when I look above.
Trying to face the fact that you've entered a better home;
sometimes I feel empty and so all alone.
I'd give anything to see you smile again,
you were more than just a grandfather,
you were my best friend.
I respected your presence and all that you said,
you've influenced me deeply, with the life you've led.
Even though you're gone, I want you here,
but I know you're enjoying the peacefulness we fear.
Even though I have to stay strong and true to my game,
my love for you will always maintain.
I'm Missing You

Granddads

Mari Evans

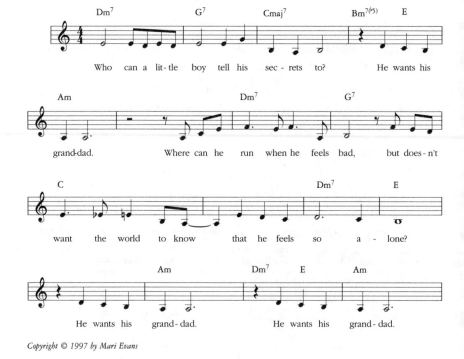

Copyright © 1997 by Mari Evans

Mike

Lois Berg

Grandpa came to live with us after Grandma passed. He was seventy-eight then, had graying red hair and a mustache, and soaking wet couldn't have weighed more than 130 pounds. It wasn't that he watched his weight or anything like that, he just had one of those metabolisms that burn weight off. Grandpa could eat, although he didn't live to eat, the way Daddy and I did, but ate to live, and ate faster than anybody I had ever seen. He said that, because he was the youngest of thirteen, when food hit the table you had to eat it all fast before somebody else got it.

One of the stories told—his family's claim to fame or immortality—was that his eldest brother was a Pinkerton guard on Lincoln's Last Train. I only knew two of his youngest sisters, for they were the only ones left. There was Aunt Tilly, who always wore fresh flowers in her hat, and Aunt Sadie, who was the mother of Mina and Lala, two second cousins who always looked like the villainesses from a Walt Disney movie. Grandpa would explain his family like this: "You can pick your friends, but family is a given."

Everyone referred to him as "Little Mean Mike." You didn't want to cross my grandfather, but if he was on your side, he'd be there for life. Mike retired at fifty to be with Grandma, who had a weak heart. After her death, he was lonesome and a little bored, so he used to go into work with my uncle Ira. He became kind of an office boy, running errands, getting lunch, going to the bank, etc. This gave him purpose and I think prolonged his life.

Toward the end of his life, my grandfather developed selective hearing. Like a child, he'd hear only the things that he wanted to. The radio or TV volume was almost always on high when he was listening, but if you whispered his name a room away, he, for certain, would hear that and come running. There are specific pictures that we have in our minds' photo albums, and one of mine is of Grandpa sitting just a few feet from the console TV set, the volume up and rocking the house, and his fists clutched or pounding the chair or each other.

Every Tuesday night he and my father would watch the fights from St. Nicholas Arena in upper Manhattan. My father and his brothers once owned a boxer. They had shares in the training, upkeep, and fees of an Irish-American middleweight. So, as in a ritual, my grandfather and my dad would move the captain's chairs from the front bay window to right in front of our RCA thirteen-inch black-and-white and turn on WPIX. The announcers' voices would echo through every nook and cranny of the house as they called each round's actions. Between rounds or fights my dad and grandfather would argue about everything and anything but especially sports. Both men, or shall I say most men, remember sports statistics the way women remember childbirth.

Like my father, Mike was meticulous in his grooming and his dress. We shared a bathroom after he came to live with us, and every morning he'd seem to take forever getting ready to go to his job in the city. I never understood this: he would bathe at night, so how long could it take to comb thinning hair or shave? Sometimes, if it was the weekend, he would let me watch him shave, using a straight razor and mixing his own cream in a cup from a special bar of shaving soap. He had a leather strop that attached to the towel rack under the bathroom window to sharpen his razor, and a bristled brush that felt like velvet when dry. While he shaved, he would tell me stories about his brothers and sisters, some funny, some sad. Then, when he was done, he would let me pour some lavender-scented lotion into his cupped hands, which he'd apply to his face and neck. I still connect the smell of lavender to those mornings in the bathroom.

Grandpa loved our dog, Rebbie, and on the weekends would take him for long walks in the neighborhood. But he also teased the dog mercilessly, and sometimes, when Rebbie had had enough, he would growl at Grandpa as if to say, "If you don't stop, old man, I'll bite you." Grandpa loved his peppermint schnapps with a little seltzer water, which we would get delivered by the soda man. Almost every night—before turning in, as he called it—he would mix himself a stiff one—another expression of his—and toast his beloved wife, Francis. One night four years after he moved in, he took his bath, came down in his pajamas, robe, and slippers, and mixed himself his usual. He went upstairs to sleep then, but never woke up. After eighty-two years of life, fifty-eight years of marriage, children, grandchildren, and I don't know how many arguments with my father, Grandpa had had enough.

The Satisfaction Coal Company

Rita Dove

1.

What to do with a day.
Leaf through *Jet*. Watch T.V.
Freezing on the porch
but he goes anyhow, snow too high
for a walk, the ice treacherous.
Inside, the gas heater takes care of itself;
he doesn't even notice being warm.

Everyone says he looks great.
Across the street a drunk stands smiling
at something carved in a tree.
The new neighbor with the floating hips
scoots out to get the mail
and waves once, brightly,
storm door clipping her heel on the way in.

2.

Twice a week he had taken the bus down Glendale hill
to the corner of Market. Slipped through
the alley by the canal and let himself in.
Started to sweep
with terrible care, like a woman
brushing shine into her hair,
same motion, same lullaby.
No curtains—the cop on the beat
stopped outside once in the hour
to swing his billy club and glare.

It was better on Saturdays
when the children came along:
he mopped while they emptied
ashtrays, clang of glass on metal,
then a dry scutter. Next they counted
nailheads studding the leather cushions.
Thirty-four! they shouted,
that was the year and
they found it mighty amusing.

But during the week he noticed more—
lights when they gushed or dimmed
at the Portage Hotel, the 10:32
picking up speed past the B & O switchyard,
floorboards trembling and the explosive
kachook kachook kachook kachook
and the oiled rails ticking underneath.

3.

They were poor then but everyone had been poor.
He hadn't minded the sweeping,
just the thought of it—like now
when people ask him what he's thinking
and he says *I'm listening.*

Those nights walking home alone,
the bucket of coal scraps banging his knee,
he'd hear a roaring furnace
with its dry, familiar heat. Now the nights
take care of themselves—as for the days,
there is the canary's sweet curdled song,
the wino smiling through his dribble.
Past the hill, past the gorge
choked with wild sumac in summer,
the corner has been upgraded.
Still, he'd like to go down there someday
to stand for a while, and get warm.

Grandpa Beavers

Consuelo Harris

Grandpa enjoyed telling and listening to stories. I remember a summer when I was a teenager, a warm evening when he and Grandma and I sat rocking on their front porch laughing while he told a story about a drunken frog. He laughed even harder when he told about the incense pot being left in the foyer by the altar boy because it was "too damn hot."

Grandpa loved to laugh, and his sense of humor was infectious. He had a way of making people feel very comfortable; you could be sure of laughing at least once during a conversation with him. We laughed a lot that night, but at some point the mood changed and he held us breathless as he told the story of Nat Turner.

There were other nights and other stories, but one . . . I wish I had been curious enough, attentive enough, wise enough, to ask him to tell his own story—in his own inimitable style. Now, instead, I must rely on a few documented facts, family stories, and the collective memories of my brothers, cousins, and a few extended-family members.

We have vivid, shared memories of Grandpa on his frequent

jaunts around town and even into the country, complete with tilted homburg or straw hat and bow tie, sporting his walking cane in such a style that you knew it *was* for style. Much as he did love to walk, he also enjoyed weekly Sunday-afternoon drives with his oldest son, wife, and granddaughter. The only problem was that Grandpa puzzled over "why this thing goes dry every time I get in it." The rides were worth the five-dollar cost of the gas. Frequently the route took them past the segregated public schools in the city and county, invariably eliciting the sardonic observation: "There's Old [Separate but] Equal."

William Edward Beavers, born November 28, 1875, was the oldest of six boys and eight girls born to William and Mary Wilson Beavers in Pittsylvania County, Virginia.

Twenty years later, he was listed as "missing" on the Lincoln University (Pennsylvania) student roster. Sometime after Lincoln, he taught school—for a day. He said that one boy, much bigger than he, challenged him to a fight, so he quit. (He stayed out of family fights, too, and got along well with everyone.) Maybe it was after his less-than-illustrious teaching career that he took the test for railway postal clerks, scoring the highest marks ever made up to then. He was hired, and rode the rails sorting mail until he retired. For the rest of his life, he could track the trains as they rumbled by, identifying the number by the whistles and the time of day, whether the train was right on time or "running behind," according to his ever-present pocket watch.

On October 1, 1900, William married Lena Lanier, the only daughter of Martha and King David Lanier. Once, after Grandma had one-upped "Will" again, he turned to me, a totally innocent bystander, and explained that when he'd asked her father for permission to marry her, it was granted with a warning. King David said: "You're welcome to her. I've tried to tame her, but have never been able to do it. I wish you luck." Grandpa laughed and shook his head. He must have understood that, with five boys and five girls to rear (my mother was the sixth child), Lena needed all that fire and spirit.

Grandpa's days as a postal clerk were over before I knew anything about them. I remember him as a grocery-store clerk. More than a clerk, really: he was the owner of Beavers Grocery, No. 1; No. 2 being owned by his son. "The Store," as we called it, was the neighborhood gathering place morning, noon, and night for young and old alike. Wintertime, the shoppers and the sitters gathered round the coal stove, atop which was almost always a big pot of beans, soup, or stew that he shared equally with family and friends. We later discovered the limits of his culinary skills when he cooked for Grandma during an illness. Every morning he would solicitously inquire what she'd like for breakfast, and every morning he served her a bowl of oatmeal. I suspect that, once she was well again, she never ate another bowl of oatmeal.

Come spring—through summer and fall—the gathering, the checkers and Chinese-checkers games, and the storytelling (teasing, signifying, and lying) moved out to the porch and surrounding yard. Hardly a day passed without a raucous, hotly contested game of baseball, football, or marbles in the yard.

Some customers never seemed to learn what the grandchildren figured out, after being caught off guard a few times, which was how to greet (or not greet) Grandpa. "Well, how are you today?" he would ask. The reply, "Pretty good, thanks," would be countered with the response, "If you're pretty and good, you're doing just fine." Pity the poor unwitting soul who, perhaps expecting some small measure of sympathy, admitted to feeling bad. The retort would be, "I hope you don't feel as bad as you look, 'cause you look mighty bad," followed by shouts of laughter all around. A child politely professing to be ten years old (or whatever age) would be challenged "because nobody could get that ugly in just ten years." In fact, he teased almost everyone, calling him or her Lee—"Ug-lee."

Maybe the customers really did get the last laugh. Despite promises to "see you on Saturday," which was the same thing Grandpa always said in church when the ushers passed the collection plate, quite a few of them never got out of the debit column on their page in his credit books. I surely owed him plenty of thanks for the many Almond Joys he let me take from the candy case.

Far more than for the candy I was given as an adolescent, I am endlessly grateful for the name he gave me as an infant. Fortunately, Mama and Daddy accepted his recommendation that Consuelo, from Mama, and Lanier, from Grandma, was much better than the name originally chosen—which does not bear repeating. His choices do bear repeating, and so my daughter has the same middle name as her grandmother and my son has mine.

My earliest memory of anything is being at my grandparents' home when I was two, sitting in my own orange-crate chair with my own books stored beneath the seat. Just like Grandpa, we are a family of insatiable, incessant readers. After Grandma's eyesight failed, Grandpa indulged her need for the news by reading the daily papers to her.

Grandpa was the only person I've ever known to subscribe to *The Christian Science Monitor.* Despite his being clerk of session of the Presbyterian church immediately adjacent to his home, he studied and adhered to the principles of Christian Science. Although no one can remember that he ever attended any meetings, he communicated with other Christian Scientists. Perhaps he taught himself to type for that reason, taping blank paper over each letter on his cumbersome Underwood in order to memorize the keyboard.

Other newspapers, books, and magazines were piled dangerously high in his bedroom, barely leaving him a path to the bed; but more than any of these, he read his Bible—daily, constantly—over and over and over. Had he been a contestant on the infamous *$64,000 Question* quiz show, they could have saved themselves the scandal of a fixed game in the Bible category, because he honestly knew all the answers.

The solid, comfortable brick house that Grandpa erected with his own hands was carefully, thoughtfully planned. The L-shaped concrete front porch was adequate for welcoming family, neighbors, and friends, but the back of the house demanded two porches. On the second-floor porch he screened in enough space for two summer sleep-out beds. Enclosed on the downstairs porch was the pantry where Grandma stored the summer's canning and her legendary homemade grape and dandelion wine. There was still plenty of room for the watermelon feasts.

The watermelon man always completed his summer-afternoon rounds with melons fresh from the field at Grandpa's. Whatever was left on the wagon went into waiting galvanized tubs of ice setting on the back porch. After dinner, grand- and neighbor children would eagerly wait to be called from nightly games for watermelon time. Grandpa swore that he could fill up on watermelon, but never get enough of it, so one melon was always reserved for him. But there were enough slices for all, and more for those who imagined that they had his capacity. Few of the seeds aimed at the tin tubs made their marks, most becoming missiles in the ensuing seed-spitting contests. The yard beside "The Store" even had its own randomly seeded watermelon patch.

Fifty years ago, watermelon was not often among the mid-winter fresh-produce selections at the A&P or at Piggly-Wiggly. His great watermelon obsession prompted Grandpa to seek a remedy for this shortcoming. At the end of summer one year, he selected a choice specimen, stored it in the big re-frigerated case at the back of the store, and waited for the cold to set in. On a sunny late-winter afternoon, with a newspaper photographer's camera aimed at him, he anxiously retrieved the melon, gave it a practiced thump, then made the cut. The experiment was successful and deliciously satisfying.

Our most treasured family photograph is the portrait of Grandpa as a young man that hung over the living-room mantel. For a while, the photographer displayed the handsome picture in his shop window, but removed it after a white customer demanded to know why he had "that nigger's picture in the window." All of the grandchildren now covet that portrait to hang prominently in our homes. Today's technology will enable us to work this out in a "grandfatherly way"— without family fights. Reproduction science being what it is, we can all have Grandpa with us, just as we have always had.

SO IT STOOD

Of Grandfathers and Granddaughters

Hilbert H. Campbell

One of my grandfathers was dead before I was born. The other, my mother's father, whom she called "Papa" and I was taught to call "Grandpa," I knew only slightly in the years before he died at age eighty-seven in 1943, when I was nine years old. He was a widower who did not live nearby, so I would see him only once or twice a year, when he visited, a formal, solemn presence in a black suit, invariably vested and hatted, carrying his small "grip," and wearing what I thought of as "old man's" shoes. I'm not certain, but I don't think he was able to visit at all during the last three or four years of his life, so I probably didn't see him after I was five or six.

I have retained only two specific recollections of these visits, one fuzzy, the other quite vivid. The fuzzier memory is of his falling down on the floor in a "fit" (he had epilepsy, an uncle told me many years later), and, because I do recall it only weakly, this dramatic event must have taken place when I was almost too young to retain anything in memory at all. The other memory is of his saying to me, one day when I was acting very silly, as a child of four or five will do, "They put boys who act like that in the asylum." For some reason, I remember exactly how he looked and sounded when he said it. I even have a fancied image of myself as he saw me, a small dervish with a smirk on my face, generating a lot of meaningless noise and motion.

I have no memory whatsoever of any presents or endearments from him. When I came along, he had already seen the arrival of twelve grandchildren in five different families, some of whom were more than twenty years older than I, so I couldn't have been much of a novelty. I learned in later years from my mother and from uncles and older cousins that during the more than forty years he taught in one or another one-room school he was known as a rigid disciplinarian. He was also a stern father, even attempting to continue his control over his children after they were young adults and earning their own money as, of course, one-room schoolteachers.

But he must have been a good man. I base this opinion partly on the reaction of my mother when he died. On the morning of November 11, 1943, one of her older brothers came unexpectedly into our small living room (we had no phone at the time) and said to her, "Your papa died at five-thirty this morning." Because she was normally a woman who kept an extraordinarily tight control of her outward emotions, my image of her rushing from the room, wailing and keening uncontrollably, remains today a startling one. Thirty years later, when my mother gave me her papa's Bible, which had come to her after the death of an older sister in 1968, I found in it a few jottings he had made that further humanized him a bit for me, like "The ways of God are mysterious, very, very"; or (on May 15, 1887), "I am lonely tonight. Sally [his wife] has gone to Nicholas County [to visit her sick mother]."

The fact remains, however, that my childhood was not blessed by any of the good experiences or influences that grandfathers are supposed to provide. They passed to me no traditions, told me no stories, influenced me not in any direct way that I'm aware of. I have, however, spent a good deal of my life thinking about grandfathers in the sense of "forebears" or ancestors, of the ways our fates, even our identities, continue to be influenced by who they were and what happened to them. I've been particularly fascinated by a pair of great-grandfathers who were members of Virginia Infantry regiments in the Confederate Army during the Civil War.

Josiah Anderson lived and farmed in Buckingham County in central Virginia, married sometime in 1860 (at age thirty-one), was mustered into Company C, 44th Virginia Infantry, in June 1861, and heard by letter some months later that his first child, a daughter named Sarah ("Sally"— destined to become my maternal grandmother), had been born on November 27, 1861. One year later, he went briefly AWOL and saw his daughter for the first and only time, on her first birthday. About the same time that Josiah Anderson enlisted in the 44th, James P. Bottomly (age twenty) of mountainous, newly formed Bland County in southwestern Virginia was mustered into Company F, 51st Virginia Infantry.

Both soldiers saw much action, and both lost brothers serving with them early in the war. Josiah Anderson of the 44th Virginia fought with Stonewall Jackson's troops in the Shenandoah Valley, at Second Manassas, at Sharpsburg, at Fredericksburg, and at Chancellorsville. On the early morning of May 3, 1863, the day after Jackson was mortally wounded, the 44th was nearly destroyed in the thick of the action at Chancellorsville, leaving a large number of dead and mortally wounded on the field of battle, including Sergeant Josiah Anderson.

Private James P. Bottomly, on the other hand, survived the war, having fought with the 51st Virginia in a large number of engagements from 1861 to 1865, including Fort Donelson, Chancellorsville, Missionary Ridge, New Market, Gaines' Mill (where he was wounded in the foot), Kerns-town, Winchester, Waynesboro, and many others. Along with most of the other survivors of the decimated 51st Regiment, he was captured at Waynesboro on March 2, 1865, and imprisoned at Fort Delaware. He was released June 19, 1865, after taking the oath of allegiance to the Union. After the war he married a Bland County neighbor, moved to West Virginia, and fathered a large family of girls, including my paternal grandmother. That he survived relatively intact the slaughters and maimings of so many Civil War battlefields seems little short of miraculous.

It is obvious that neither I nor a great many other folks would be who we are if James P. Bottomly had been killed in the war, an event that the odds would seem to have greatly favored. Among the hundreds of minié balls that he must have faced, all it would have taken is for one of them boring toward him to have been an inch or so to the right or left of where it actually was and—and—well, it reminds us that small, seemingly chance happenings can have long consequences.

I find it much more interesting—downright fascinating, actually—to reflect that neither would I be who I am if my great-grandfather Josiah Anderson had *not* been killed. If he had lived, he would have gone back to New Canton, Buckingham County, Virginia, resumed life with his wife, Elizabeth, and daughter, Sally, and fathered a large batch of brothers and sisters for her. Sally would have grown up, married into a local family (a Boatwright, perhaps, or a Scruggs, or a Moss, all then numerous in the New Canton area), and I would be only a partial version of myself, at best. If only the ball that killed him had been an inch or so to the right or left of where it actually was—but we've been through that already.

What actually happened after the war was quite different. In circumstances that are not recorded (although potential husbands and economic resources must both have been scarce), Elizabeth Anderson met and married an older widower and moved with him to his home 150 miles to the northwest, in Nicholas County, West Virginia. Here Sally grew up without brothers or sisters, went to the local one-room school, courted and married the teacher (my "grandpa" McClung, with whom this story began). Sometime in the 1950s, a very old man that everybody called "Uncle Bob"— who had been a pupil in the school at the time—told me, chuckling all the while, that the courting had progressed during school hours by passing notes back and forth in Sally's geography book. A family story that I heard early in life is that, when they got married (on March 22, 1881), because "Good Charley," the preacher who was to marry them, had the measles, they were married through a window. The rest, as they say, is history.

But my primary association with the idea of "grandfathers"—and the most pleasant—is that I have now been a grandfather myself for about seven years. My two granddaughters, sisters named Tiffany and Tabitha, were born in 1990 and 1994. As much as I would like to claim some startlingly original quality for this relationship, I'm afraid that I have proved to be an entirely sentimental and conventional grandparent. I tell people who don't want to hear it what joys grandchildren are, I take too many bad snapshots, I pick up too many ill-chosen toys and presents for addition to the stacks and stacks they already have. I find myself identifying with the man in the TV commercial who links his drinking of a dietary supplement to keeping his promise to a granddaughter. "Will you come to my wedding?" she asks. "I'll be there," he responds, smilingly tipping up the can of Ensure for another swig.

So I, too, want to live long enough to go to their weddings. Or, if not, at least long enough to share in some way whatever joys, successes, and celebrations may be part of their young lives. I've been fortunate that they live nearby; and, without my really thinking about it, they already have become very much a part of my life. I "baby-sit," and sometimes I color with them. We play tag or "Mother, May I," and I push them on the swings. I play word games with Tiffany, who has been learning the alphabet and the spelling of simple words. Each of these occasions is the more meaningful because I and other grandfathers have lived long enough to know how fragile precious things are, how swiftly time passes, and how this very transitory nature of things makes them more valuable.

Although I know I can't determine who my granddaughters will become or shield them from the uncertainties of the hard and sometimes treacherous world that we all must live in, I nevertheless try to do at least some small things that they might later appreciate or that might help them in the future: I have stashed away a number of newspapers and magazines dating from the time (day, week) of their births, hoping that someday they might find these items of interest. I order for them each year proof and mint sets of United States coins. And each Christmas their grandmother and I give them savings bonds, hoping that these might later help in some small way with their educations.

They give me so much pleasure just by being there that I ponder sometimes the question of whether and what I might be able to give back. Will I, for example, ever teach them anything worthwhile? Knowing that we all learn things only when we have a desire or a need to learn them, I'll probably teach them something only if I'm around when they develop a need or a curiosity for something I know about. I'm sure only that I'll be falling all over myself with willingness if one of them does ever ask me a question about our ancestors, or about what my childhood was like several decades before their own.

How to conclude this report from inside grandfatherhood? What's it really like to be "Granddaddy"? Like anything else, it is what you make of it. But take it from one who has been there: it can be a goodly, a blessed, and a joyful estate.

My Grandpa Leo

Leo Kamell Sacks

Leo Kamell was proud and strong and generous and trust-
ing. He had big black eyes and bushy hair and furry eye-
brows, just like mine. He loved excitement and adventure,
and he gave those gifts to me. I am Leo Kamell's first grandson, Leo Kamell Sacks.

Leo lived in a steeply sloped house that rose like a castle
from 124 Elliot Avenue in Yonkers, New York. His work-
day began after dark when he drove his big red Buick down
the West Side Highway into the mighty wind off the
Hudson River. At the Washington Market near Fourteenth
Street he bought hundreds of pounds of fruits and vegetables
for MAK Fruit, his produce company. MAK supplied the
ripest pears, the juiciest peaches, and the crunchiest apples
to twenty-six grocery stores in Westchester County. MAK
also fed a few convents and monasteries and the lost souls at
Sing Sing prison. Leo believed everyone deserved to eat well.

Leo loved to buy in bulk but he savored the process of un-
wrapping each smooth piece of fruit and shaping pyramids

LEO KAMELL

that defied gravity. While he handled the fruit, Leo trusted his partners, Marks and Aronowitz, to run the business. MAK Fruit boomed during the depths of the Depression, because Leo fought to give poor people the best prices and let them keep their dignity.

The smell of onions and garlic and overripe fruit followed Leo everywhere. When he came home from Fight Night at the old Madison Square Garden, he brought the manly odors of cigar smoke and gasoline with him. Leo loved the fighters' instincts and their electric speed. He loved the buzz of the Garden, the flash and swagger of the flyweights, the brutish power of the heavyweights, the rhythms of the ring.

He always had the best seats at the fights. Strangers thought Leo looked like Max Baer, the undisputed heavyweight champ in 1934. He got a kick out of that. Baer wore the Star of David sewn on his trunks and Leo liked that ethnic imagery, although generally Leo was more spiritual than religious. Religious people are afraid of hell, he reasoned; spiritual people have already been there.

In 1908, Leo, a born fighter, slipped out of the family house in Trieste, the ancient port on Italy's southern coast. Eleven-year-old Leo stowed away on a steamship with his cousin Abe and came to America.

The two cousins disappeared into the Lower East Side. It was a daily race for bread and a place to dream at night. Leo and Abe survived on guts and instinct and faith in the God that saw them across the sea. There must have been an angel of mercy to feed their hungry hearts, to help them face the unknown.

Leo had a pushcart piled high with cucumbers for pick-ling when he was introduced to Barbara Schneiderman. She had sailed to the States with her father and arrived in New York Harbor when she was twelve. She came from the Ukraine, in the cold core of Russia. Her friends called her Bobby, and when other girls were skipping rope, Bobby was keeping house.

She had curly hair and baby-soft skin and she learned English faster than the boys in her class. She worked fourteen hours a day, hunched over a noisy sewing machine in a dirty sweatshop in lower Manhattan. She walked a hundred blocks home to save a nickel; she slept on a bed of four chairs.

Leo brought Bobby flowers, chocolates, and shy smiles. Her father, Israel, was outraged. He thought all Italians were killers. *"Run away from him!"* Israel demanded. "To where?" Bobby questioned. *"To Boston!"* he shouted. My mom laughs when she tells this story. Israel must have thought Boston was very far away.

In Bobby's arms, Leo was a teddy bear. When Israel saw they were in love, that Leo would be a good provider, he con-gratulated them on their wedding day.

Leo had the nervy blood of a gambler. He was so good at pinochle that a professional cheat once said they could make a bundle. But Leo turned the cheat down because he loved the game. Leo also played the ponies at Yonkers Raceway, tipping his fedora at the ticket window whether he was lay-ing bets or cashing in. He bought a mare who came up lame on her first race. When she was put down, Leo took off his hat and stared at the ground. Bad luck.

He was a demanding boss, but Leo inspired great loyalty. When MAK's warehouse opened, the men who drove the delivery trucks papered the walls with red-and-white bunting. They brought their families to the picnic Leo threw every summer. They liked to kibitz with him. But Leo's partners mistook Leo's kindness for weakness.

In Westchester County, the mobsters who controlled the trash collectors' union in the early forties could be very persuasive. They determined who would haul MAK's trash, and when, and they let Leo know it. At the same time, a new district attorney—Tom Dewey—was making a name for himself as New York's top gangbuster. Dewey felt it was in MAK's best interest to cooperate with his investigation of the union, so he sent two men in trench coats to have a chat with my mom, a little girl carrying her books on her way home from school.

Leo's idea of trouble was exotic fruit out of season, like fresh peaches in January. On the outside he looked cool as a cucumber, only now there were wise guys calling his house. *"We know where you live. We know what time your children come home from school."* Leo was being pulled from two sides, but instinctively played them both against the middle. (For years, he gave money to the Democrats and the Republicans, and neither one knew; in his heart of hearts, he was a Liberal, anyway.)

The stress eventually took its toll. One night, after dinner, Leo had chest pains. He climbed the stairs to his bedroom and collapsed. Bobby rushed to his bedside, reassuring and comforting him. My grandpa Leo Kamell died of cardiac arrest. He was fifty-six years old.

During the seven days of mourning, Louie D'Aguarde was among the first to pay his respect. Louis worked for MAK, because Leo had given him a job after the stock market crashed and his family was destitute. Leo naturally understood the flow of power and politics; he gave his congressman five thousand dollars to make him a U.S. citizen. My mom whispers that to me now as if she's afraid someone might get in trouble. Then she smiles. She knows better.

Leo left Bobby with only one store; his business collapsed as quickly as it had grown. Bobby went back to being a seamstress. This beautiful woman who was tough as nails was alone now.

I never told anyone that Leo would visit me on long afternoons, motioning where to mow the lawn or trim the hedge. He'd lead me down to the cellar, lugging wooden crates of Cott's cherry soda and Two Cents Plain. That musty cellar, where he buried ten thousand dollars in small bills. By the time Bobby remembered, the serial numbers were practically invisible.

When I received my middle school diploma in 1968 and the principal announced Leo Sacks instead of Leo Kamell Sacks, Bobby asked me if I was ashamed of my middle name. It didn't seem like a very big deal, but I know now that it was. I know because I was Bobby's protector when we walked in the park holding hands. In my white shirt and bow tie, I escorted her on the breezy boardwalk in Long Beach, on Long Island. My pompadour was piled high with Brylcreem and all the ladies said, "What a nice little man you have, Bobby."

She taught me how to play canasta at the kitchen table for a penny a point. We'd peel orange slices into eighths, the way she liked them. Then we'd watch Merv Griffin chat with Zsa Zsa Gabor and I'd watch her eyes water as Steve Lawrence sang "Yesterday" on the Mike Douglas show. I'm listening to the song today, only now in the vulnerable voice of Marvin Gaye. I never met my grandpa Leo, yet I know we absolutely adore each other.

For My Grandfather

🌀🌀🌀

Father Joseph Brown

when I was your age

                            he said

there were books I loved to read

will you learn and find and read

them

               for me

                      of course yes today and

tomorrow if

                  need

                        be all the fire

a promise feeds upon

                          I will yet

find and learn and love

what your blind eyes

                     can no longer

thaw

meanly then so small and foolish

were the words

what does this

spell and this and this

of coarse

small pebbles falling from the lips this

path was finely

finally

stretched out

finding me

here

still sighting

the adventure

you would never read again

old man

be patient as I turn

yet another

page

So Many Memories

❧❧❧

Twanda Black Dudley

Arthur Taylor, Sr., was born August 31, 1921, in Crescent City, Florida, to parents who worked the land, so we never got the stories of how he walked ten miles to school in the freezing snow. But we did hear of his days in the orange groves—that was the main source of work in those days. Granddaddy grew up and after high school joined the Navy. As a decorated officer in the Second World War, he traveled all over the South Pacific (we still have his steamer trunk with all of the stickers on it). He told us many stories of his days in "hell," including how the front of the vehicle that he was driving was blown off in a raid—complete with pictures and bad feet that my grandmother had to care for, for the rest of their days together.

Granddaddy married my grandmother in Tampa, Florida, on his second go-round, and they produced one daughter, but my grandmother had already given birth to eight children before this last one. No—there were never nine children in the house at once, because at least three were grown

ARTHUR TAYLOR, SR.

and on their own. I remember this huge two-story house by the railroad tracks that shook when the trains passed by. My brother and I spent a lot of time there. My grandfather always had a favorite chair in each room that no one could sit in but him. And if you were foolish enough to get caught sitting in his chair—watch out!

Granddaddy moved back to Crescent City and made his living growing ferns on twenty acres of land left to him by his father (his mother still lived on the land). He'd rise early, usually at 4:30 A.M., and collect his workers for a day's work. This included his wife, children, and mother, who were all responsible for certain areas in the fern patch. During our annual two-month summer visits when we were old enough to go in the field, we had to pull the weeds and grass between the rows. We were paid, mind you—a whopping fifty cents a week.

Granddaddy always wore a cap over his shiny donut head (you know, the clean dome on top with just a bit of fine hair on the sides) to protect him from the sun, he'd say. In my twenty-eight years of knowing him, I had never seen him with hair on his head. The big rifle he carried over his shoulder was for the snakes and armadillos who were daily visitors in the field. We'd always run when we'd hear the rifle go off, because there'd always be an exciting story behind every blast.

We were all in awe of Granddaddy (and a little scared). He always kept everything in order, especially us grandchildren. We had to eat all of our meals together, even the occasional evening snack. The television had to go off at a certain time each night—no late movies and no talking in bed unless we wanted to feel the big brown strap that would beat us for old and new. After making the quota for the week, making his route through Tampa to all of his florists (which usually took four or five hours), and collecting his hard-earned money, Granddad would come back home relaxed, happy, and whistling a jazzy tune. He was a world-class whistler and could whistle any tune just like the birds we heard every morning outside our window.

Granddad would "get clean," as he called it, with his lime-green or cornflower-blue polyester pullover (much like the ones worn today) and a pair of Sansabelt slacks with the Spock boots with the square toes (he had three colors: brown, black, and burgundy) and his sporty dress cap. He'd be sharp as a tack! He'd take us all into town and buy us candy and all that other incidental stuff needed for the house, like food and toiletries.

As we waited for Grandmom to finish dinner, which usually consisted of some kind of bean and rice, Granddad would sit in the Florida room in his favorite chair blowing smoke rings for us to try and put our fingers through. He'd listen to his Coltrane, Charlie Parker, Charles Mingus, Sarah Vaughan, Etta James, and Billie Holiday albums (all wax, of course—and we were not allowed to touch them). I can see him now sitting in that chair bobbing his head up and down, popping his fingers, and saying, "Now, that's jazz, man, those cats are cool!," and beginning to whistle as though he were sitting in on a live jam session. My grandmother still has those albums (well protected, I might add), even though Granddad's been gone since Mother's Day, 1990. I hope to inherit those albums someday.

Then There Were Sundays

Danella Carter

Then there were Sundays, my favorite day of the week, thanks to Grandpop Cothran. Grandpop was a Sunday cook, a self-taught amateur chef whose meals ranged from oxtail stew to coq au vin. Sundays would officially begin around 6:30 A.M., when Grandpop lulled us out of bed with stirring melodies of gospel music, which would play on the radio throughout the day. The air was thick with the smell of biscuits baking and coffee (off-limits to us, of course) brewing in the pot. By seven, we were all at the table eating portions of baked shad with crisp sweet onion and eggs sunny-side up.

In the afternoon, Grandpop would begin preparing Sunday dinner. I loved watching him work. The kitchen was very large, and yet Grandpop seemed to tower over everything. He wore a white paneled apron with a small cloth tucked under the sash, which he used to wipe off his worktable, the stove, and the sides of pots whenever any-thing boiled over. On the Formica counter were the usual props: a chopping block, Ginsu knives, and a small jelly jar half filled with iced Canadian whiskey. (Grandpop is now a very active churchgoer and has become a solid teetotaler.) Grandpop was a slow, methodical cook who abhorred new-fangled gadgets like the Veg-O-Matic, preferring instead the concentration that comes from dicing and grating by hand.

I trusted Grandpop's judgment in food; he was the only person who could get me to eat macaroni and cheese, but that was because he deviated from the usual milk-and-cheese sludge I'd never acquired a taste for. He'd toss the macaroni in a little butter, with mushrooms, herbs, and a cheese I now recognize as Parmesan. Then he'd carefully craft a top layer with sliced tomatoes, crown it with a con-genial mixture of shallots, celery, and bread crumbs, and broil it for five minutes. Scrumptious! Another one of my favorites was his corn pudding: freshly hulled corn, minced green bell peppers, and red chili peppers suspended in an airy custard base.

Grandpop wasn't much of a dessert maker, but he topped off each meal by washing all the dishes. And though Grandmom Cothran wasn't much for cooking, she always came through with after-dinner treats like fresh-picked grapes or banana pudding (remember the kind with vanilla wafers along the sides?). Grandmom is no longer with us, but memories abound of her great skills as a painter, milliner, and weaver.

Here is one of Grandpop's recipes:

Grandpop's Macaroni and Cheese

My sister Diana and I split on the issue of macaroni and cheese; she preferred Grandmom's, which was elegant in its own right—but a bit too cheesy—while I leaned toward Grandpop's lighter version. I'm not certain if Grandpop used ricotta cheese, but I find it a pleasurable addition.

4 cups macaroni, cooked al dente
1 cup sliced mushrooms
¼ cup chopped shallots
2 stalks celery, finely chopped
2 teaspoons butter, melted
1½ cups evaporated skim milk
¾ cup part-skim ricotta cheese
1 egg, beaten
1 red bell pepper, seeded and diced
1 tablespoon minced tarragon
1 teaspoon salt
½ teaspoon freshly ground white pepper
1 teaspoon ground tapioca
¼ teaspoon nutmeg
¼ cup grated Parmesan cheese
1 teaspoon grated lemon zest
¼ cup bread crumbs
2 tomatoes

Preheat the oven to 350 degrees. Butter a large soufflé dish and set aside. Put cooked macaroni in a large mixing bowl. Sauté mushrooms, shallots, and celery in butter over low heat for 5 minutes, until cooked, but firm; add to macaroni and toss. Combine milk, ricotta, egg, bell pepper, tarragon, salt, pepper, tapioca, and nutmeg, and beat until well blended. Pour mixture over the macaroni and transfer macaroni to the soufflé dish. In a small bowl, combine Parmesan, lemon zest, and bread crumbs. Slice tomato thinly and pat dry. Starting from the center, form a spiral across the top of the macaroni with the tomatoes, overlapping if necessary. Sprinkle crumb mixture on top and bake for 35 minutes, until golden brown on top. *Serves 8.*

His Spirit Is Still

The Honorable Ed Vaughn

I was born in Abbeville, but when I was two my family moved to Dothan, Alabama, just thirty miles away. I was born in Granddaddy Charlie's house. I always remembered Granddaddy Charlie as a strict disciplinarian, the best carpenter in the world, and the owner of Charlie Vaughn's grocery store. He never failed to give me a handful of candy when I visited the store.

I thought my granddaddy was the most powerful and smartest man in the world. He was my role model. His grocery store was next door to his house, the church of which he was pastor across the street.

I grew up in the 1940s. All the skilled tradesmen were black (the legacy of Tuskegee University, just thirty miles from Abbeville), but my granddaddy was a master carpenter! He could make blueprints and supervised the building of half the homes in Abbeville.

My granddaddy built a new addition on our first house in Dothan—new kitchen, dining room, den, and a bathroom, inside! I watched that man build that addition and was amazed at his great skill. The addition is still part of my childhood home and still looks good. My granddaddy was a handsome man with the energy of a dozen people.

His spirit is still part of my life today. I am now engaged in the biggest political fight of my life, my campaign for mayor of Detroit. My campaign office is bugged, I have been denied the right to speak at the 11th Police Precinct, and two of my campaign workers were just arrested for passing out my literature on a public street. I am still fighting for my place in the sun, but not fighting by myself. The spirit of Charlie Vaughn stands at the head of all my ancestors, giving me the strength to continue the struggle.

My grandfather on my mother's side, Frank White, died before I was born. We have a big picture of him lying in his casket. He too was born in Alabama, near Eufaula. His father, a white plantation owner, raped his mother and always denied his son. Granddaddy Frank tried to kill his father but was unable to carry it out. He did kill his father's prize goat, and then ran away. He followed the horse-race circuit across America, eventually ending up in Abbeville, where he married my grandmother Ida Hogan White.

I was told my granddaddy Frank, who worked in a bank, would overhear whites talking and on many occasions would warn black citizens when whites were planning to kill them. He was a very courageous man, and his spirit lived on in my grandmother Ida. She was a wealthy woman, by small-town standards. She sold meat (slaughtering her own hogs), canned and sold fruits and vegetables, churned butter, sold chickens and eggs, sold chalk (a substance found in the red dirt of Alabama that people loved to eat), took in five washings. She had more money than the white families she washed for.

Every Monday we went to the natural spring on her land to help her wash clothes. My grandmother was the only black person in town who purchased new cars. She always paid cash for them, to the amazement of the white salesmen.

My grandmother told me that she would never remarry and that she was so industrious because she wanted to carry on the work started by my granddaddy Frank White. She was inspired by him, and I am inspired by both of them.

These memories of my grandfathers are shared in love and respect for the historic struggles of my family, my people, and my extended human family.

Liberties

(for Dianne)

Opal Moore

Papa drove a taxi cab
on weekdays, preached on Sundays,
gave his grandoffspring nickels,
and a silver dollar on birthdays.

Took liberties as only men could do,
like spooning white ice cream
right from the carton
to his mouth.

Promised my sister rare coins:
Indian-head, buffalo, walking liberty,
set aside from what he took in tips
and tipping out with sideline women.

Promised to die
and leave my sister a white wealth
of coin, rare, bitten.
Died.

Left this: a cigar box of blackened coin
his widow traded for funeral potatoes, peas,
chicken to fry, cornbread and greens,
and a box to lay him in.

Sister got new Lincoln pennies,
enough for the white ice cream she
spooned determined from the pint
to her mouth. She ate the coolness of his spirit.
It was the liberty coin he left her.

This Is His Love

Nefertitti Rhodes

My cousins have always thought my grandfather looks like Richard Pryor. His mother was half Cherokee Indian, and you can see the sharp definitions in his cheekbones, characteristic of Native Americans. Although he's very handsome, it's a long-standing joke that when he lets his hair grow too long, which occurs more often than not, he looks like a Don King wannabe. Looking at his hands and face, you can tell that he has spent many long hours in the fields of the hot California sun. Yet, when he undresses, his arms and legs are a golden yellow, like the upper part of a ripe peach. He always wears long-sleeved shirts. The only short-sleeved shirt he owns is the one my sisters and I bought him one year for Father's Day. It had a red background, with a tropical print. He showed his better judgment by never wearing that shirt.

He was born and raised in Palestine, Texas, but moved to California to find a job and to raise six daughters and a son. Though he has vowed never to live in Texas again, he frequently makes the drive from California to Texas as if it were the three-hour drive from Fresno to Los Angeles. He loves the Dallas Cowboys, and has since before I was born. He also loved the series *Dallas.* My mother used to work the grave-yard shift. She would drop us off at our grandparents' just before 9:00 P.M. Sitting in the den on Thursday nights with-out fail, my grandparents, my sisters, and I would sit down for our evening fix of *Falcon Crest* and *Dallas.*

My grandfather is as diverse as the images and memories that anyone could conjure up of his or her own grandfather. He's a preacher, but he doesn't go to church every Sunday. He plays the guitar—music that sounds like the blues—but he'd never set foot inside of a blues club. For health reasons, he doesn't eat any red meat, but he has smoked pipes and cigars and chewed tobacco for many years. He's been retired for years, but he is always working: repairing cars; selling watermelons, Christmas trees, cars; and plowing fields.

The earliest and fondest memories that I have of my grandfather are of him telling Brer Rabbit stories to my cousins and me as we huddled around the furnace heater. I really don't recall the stories, just the animation with which he entertained his grandchildren. When his stories get good, he walks around the room imitating the characters or people he is depicting. When it gets real good, he looks for the agreement of his audience and may say, "Ain't that right, y'all?" Usually the best thing to do is to agree with him and say yes. If you say no he'll kindly analyze all the reasons you could have possibly done so, show you why you're wrong, and keep working the audience until there's no one left but you in the room and then you finally say yes just so the conversation can come to an end.

He is the only male role model I had while growing up as a girl. When other men (father, stepfather, uncles, etc.) came and went, he remained a constant. "Diddy" is the name his children call him. His eldest daughter couldn't pronounce "Daddy," so "Diddy" is what stuck. When his daughters ran out of gas or had flat tires, they would call Diddy, confident that two things would occur: that Diddy would bail them successfully out of their bad situation, and that he would curse them out for not being better prepared. My aunts were notorious for never looking at the gas levels, or the temperature gauges in their cars.

My grandfather is a man from an era when men were the sole protectors of their families. If people violated or invaded a space that did not belong to them, he made sure the wrongs were rectified. I recall having our bikes stolen from the front yard several times. My grandfather would gather us in his truck, and we would go driving around the neighborhood until we saw our bikes, and he would talk to the people who had stolen them. We never heard the words that were exchanged, but we always knew that, if we saw the bike, it would be coming home with us.

There used to be a time in our family when he commanded all of the attention. With age, however, his status as the sole patriarch has declined. His children and grandchildren used to listen to his stories out of respect. But they have since learned that, if they maintained their respectful postures, my grandfather would be surrounded by a captive au-

dience nearly twenty-four hours a day. Unfortunately, what
he now has to say is merely tolerated by family members,
who listen but do not hear.

My grandfather's stories can be hilarious—that is, until
you become the subject of his discussion. Every family has a
black sheep. Well, my family decided a long time ago to
have several, so that no one felt out of place. We recently
held a party for my grandparents. One black sheep—my
younger male cousin—arrived late. The entire evening, my
cousin watched his every step, trying to avoid Grandfather's
probing eye. My cousin was certain that, as Grandfather had
done in the past, he would begin to use my cousin's failures
as ammunition and ruin his evening.

Grandfather's daily conversations are filled with anecdotes,
interwoven with wit, humor, riddles, analyses, and criticisms
of the status quo. We listened for years, but as those criticisms increasingly began to point to us, our tolerance for the
stories has diminished. Unfortunately, one of the reasons his
family no longer hears him is his dogmatic approach to life.
He has great wisdom to share, but if we (his family) do not
believe or see things from his perspective and agree with all
that he has to say, we must endure words from him that not
only cut at our hearts, but also cut our ears away.

When I married two years ago, I encountered a dilemma
that I'm sure many girls from single-parent homes face—
who should give me away? My mother was more than de-
serving of the honor, and if she wasn't so traditional she
would have taken the privilege. I love Grandfather a lot and
I know that he loves me. But he has never told me that he

does. Grandfather is not an affectionate person, and I can recall few times when I have hugged him. Now the only time I do is after long absences. My grandfather was the masculine strength and constant in my life. The day I got married, I needed that strength more than at any other time before. With blurred vision, legs wobbling, and my heart pounding, I walked down the aisle with my grandfather on one arm and my biological father on the other.

It has only been since my marriage that I have reverted to my childlike awe and respect for his words and wisdom. My husband says, "Your grandfather is right. He makes a lot of sense." Outsiders do not receive the same treatment as family members, so they can truly appreciate his words of wisdom. Still, I have begun to appreciate his words once again. I have begun to understand that his criticisms are wielded in an effort to make us stronger and to shape us into visions of who he believes we should be. This is his affection. This is his love.

NINETY YEARS ON THE FLOOR

Pop Pop

Staci Shands

Lester was my mother's father. When he became a man, he changed his last name to Bāttie, just like his father changed the family name from Beatty to Baley. I don't know why my grandfather and great-grandfather changed their last names so much. I wasn't around then, and no one in my family knows why either.

I called my grandfather Pop Pop. He had two sisters. Ester was his twin, and we all called her Aunt Sis, short for Aunt Sister. Victoria was the oldest. Pop Pop was born in Pulaski, Georgia, on February 15, 1913. He married a young woman named Jose May Clark in the 1930s. They lived in the County of Bulloch, in Register, Georgia, where Pop Pop worked as a sharecropper. Wasting no time to start a family, they had three baby girls: Leatha May, Doris, and Caldean Bernice, my mother.

When Mommy was a baby, her parents got a divorce. Not knowing what to do with herself or her children, Jose left Mommy and Aunt Leatha with her mother in Register.

Mama, my great-grandmother, was a strong-spirited Cherokee who gave birth to thirteen children. She decided to raise her grandbabies along with her own kids while Jose and Aunt Doris moved to Newark, New Jersey. Around that time, Pop Pop joined the Marines; he later went overseas to fight in World War II.

When Mommy was twelve years old, Pop Pop returned to Georgia to reclaim his daughters. At first Mama wasn't having it: she wasn't ready to give up her grandbabies. But, having picked cotton since the age of five, Mommy was "sick and tired" of the South and wanted to go "up north." So Pop Pop moved his children to West Philadelphia, bought a house, and raised his daughters with a no-nonsense attitude and lots of very strict rules.

Up north, Pop Pop had a new wife named Rose, and she helped him raise Mommy and Aunt Leatha. Pop Pop had a job at a construction company. He was a deacon at the Holy Cross Church and an active Mason. On the weekends, Pop Pop would take his girls deep-sea fishing or rent a small airplane and take them flying across the Philadelphia sky. Pop Pop loved convertible cars. Whenever he put his car's top down, Mommy said, she used to like to sit on top of the backseats and enjoy the wind blowing in her face and ripping through her hair. Back then, there was no seat-belt law, so as long as she held on tight and didn't get too carried away it was okay.

In Pop Pop's house there were rules, and everyone who lived under his roof had to abide by them. The curfew was ten o'clock seven days a week—and that meant in bed at 10:00 P.M., not just arriving in the house. Sometimes he let his daughters' girlfriends stop by to visit, but their boy-friends had better not come over! Mommy said she could barely go to parties or the movies and wasn't allowed to participate in any after-school programs. Pop Pop was just strict like that.

I remember Pop Pop smelling like smoke. Mommy said it must have been his shaving cream. The stuff *stank,* but that was the only product he could use on his sensitive skin. After his children were grown and had children of their own, Pop Pop bought a huge farm in Dorothy, New Jersey. I don't know how big Pop Pop's farm was, but I do know he rented a couple of acres to a white family and still had plenty of space left over for his own use.

When I was about two or three, Mommy, Aunt Leatha, Aunt Doris, my brother, my sister, and my cousins used to pack up our cars and go to his farm for a family gathering. I liked watching Pop Pop sit high up on his tractor plowing his land. To me, he looked like a king on a throne, ruling everything and everybody. I felt so proud. He made a good living as a farmer and was very pleased with his land. He grew corn, beans, green peas, sweet potatoes, white potatoes, turnips, collard greens, mustard greens, onions, tomatoes, hot peppers, watermelons, and cantaloupes. He had lots of pigs, chickens, ducks, dogs, cats, a cow, and a white pony called Snowball he bought just for his grandchildren. I liked going with Pop Pop to feed the chickens and pigs. I was fascinated yet afraid of the animals as I watched the chickens fighting each other for food, the pigs grunting over theirs. I often played in patches of weeds I thought were some kind of exotic wildflowers. "Babe, Babe, git out those weeds befo' the ticks come out and git ya," he warned me. When I finally came out, I would be covered with the insects, and Pop Pop had to burn them slightly to get them off of me.

After each harvest, Mommy and my aunties used to cook a classic soul-food meal. There were simmered collard greens, fried chicken, mashed potatoes, corn on the cob, macaroni and cheese, grits and cheese, peas, cabbage, and my favorite, candied yams. Pop Pop always made his famous barbecue sauce. He never told anyone the recipe. One day Mommy watched him make it. He didn't know she was there. "I got it!" she boasted. "No, you don't," Pop Pop said, trying to protect his secret. He dared her to make a batch; when she did, it tasted just like his. "I told you I got it," Mommy said, pouring the sauce all over the spare ribs.

My older brother, Ricky, and cousin Danny used to wake up early in the morning and go fishing with Pop Pop, or to kill a hog so we could have barbecue later that evening. On the farm, the air was always fresh and crisp, like it was new, and the sun warm and comforting. I don't recall any rainy days. Even though I was very young, I clearly remember the good times we had with Pop Pop on his farm. Mommy can't see how I possibly could, but I do.

After Pop Pop's second heart attack, the doctor said his farm was too much for him to handle alone, so he sold it and bought a smaller one not too far away. To keep the family tradition alive, we went to the small farm and planted seeds, harvested the crops, and ate, laughed, and talked. I remember rainy days at that farm, though.

Pop Pop died on New Year's Day, 1983. Heart failure. His daughters now own the land. Since he's been gone, we haven't planted any seeds, so there's no harvest or family gathering at the farm. We don't even visit the place. Mommy and my aunties are just paying the taxes. I know it must be filled with exotic wildflowers by now.

Being on Pop Pop's farm influenced some of us to become involved in agriculture one way or another. When I was a Peace Corps volunteer in Zaire, I worked as a farmer throughout rural villages for two years. The villagers wanted to know, since I came from a grand village (New York City), how could I possibly understand anything about agriculture? I told them about Pop Pop, and they gave me an understanding nod. Ricky spent a lot of time with Pop Pop on his farm. When he went to college, he decided to major in agriculture at Alabama A&M University and later opened his own produce market in Queens, New York.

I often think about Pop Pop and his farm. I'm glad I had such an experience. My life is so different now. I can still hear him saying, "Babe, Babe, git out those weeds befo' . . ."

To My Grandfather

(Fred Stalkey Keaton, Sr.)

Hazel Clayton Harrison

In an old black-and-white photograph
You stand in your Sunday suit
Erect and solemn as a Baptist minister.

Thick handlebar mustache
Trimming your upper lip,
Eyes looking forward
As if they could see the storms
That lay ahead.

Now I know why Big Mama fell for you,
With your strong chin and spade hands
That dug up barrels of Georgia clay,
Turned them into bails of cotton,
Hands that reached up, plucked stars from the sky,
And stroked the moon.

Fred Stalkey Keaton, Sr.

You were my mother's hero.
She said angels wept, heavens parted
when you prayed.

The year before my seed sprouted
From her garden
Your long legs leaped over rainbows,
Crossed the River Jordan, and headed home to Calvary.
Now I grow in rich soil
You plowed, weeded, and planted.

I never sat on your lap,
Or called you Grandpa,
But one day we'll meet
And walk hand in hand
Into the sun.

Papa: My Grandfather Fishel

Jane Breskin Zalben

My father called my grandfather Fish, because his name was Fishel Kirshbloom. Everyone else, including me, called him Papa. He came over to the United States on the boat from Białystock, Poland, in 1920 with my mother, who was then an infant. Thank God. Or else I wouldn't be here writing this, because any family that remained died in the Holocaust.

After "Mama," my favorite grandparent, died a long and arduous death of cancer, he'd come to stay over a weekend here and there at our house. When I think of him I think of two things: him slurping his soup, and him reading from a large Haggadah at Passover seders. I would sit opposite him at our Formica kitchen table and listen, because I couldn't stand watching while he slurped the soup. As an intolerant nine-year-old, I found the sound extremely grating. I remember being so bothered by his invasion into our small ranch house in Queens that I decided to hang a rubber spider on a thin thread with Scotch tape over the door of my brother's bedroom, where Papa slept. I should have known better. Typically, after all my efforts standing on the chair anxiously waiting for him to walk into this "spider," like the old man he was, he woke up, left the room, and headed straight for the bathroom a few feet away, never noticing the string I had rigged.

He could go on for hours at our Passover seders. I mean we could be dropping like flies (I remained busy under the table, crawling between my aunts' and uncles' legs) before he finished. The Exodus from Egypt was shorter than Papa's ritual narration. He didn't skip one word of Hebrew, as brisket and matzoh balls wafted throughout the house. My uncle Morty once fell asleep and told Papa that he'd pick him up at the plagues. Sometimes I thought the eleventh plague was the egocentricity of my grandfather. Now I realize young children and old people have something in common: the world centers around them.

Papa became a vague figure in my life, except when I was dating a number of guys at once and he came to the front door and said to the twenty-year-old who ultimately became my husband, "What, another one?"

Eventually, my grandfather remarried and moved into a different apartment in the same building in Brooklyn, on Knapp Street, where we used to visit him and Mama on Sundays. I can still smell the halls in the building—boiled chicken and mothballs. Although he worked for the Post Office, through family history I have learned that, besides being a good poker player and joke teller, he was brilliant in math—something all the men in my life are—I'm not—and he was the only brother who wasn't a rabbi, so the feeling of "lack of success" and deprivation was probably passed down in the family to his three daughters, and ultimately to me.

With all the family *mishegoss* and rumblings of leftist meetings in Borough Park, when I think of it, my experience is closer to "the old country" than that of many of my friends whose parents were born here in America. Through food and Yiddish expressions, my attitude toward language and life was shaped by Mama and Papa.

Here's Papa's Passover horseradish:

Papa's Fresh Beet Horseradish

Papa pulled a nice large horseradish by its leaves from the garden. He had planted the top in the vegetable patch the year before. After a cold winter, the top grew and turned into a long horseradish. This is how he made the horseradish for the bitter herbs at the seder.

3 to 4 medium beets
2½ cups white vinegar (enough
   for soaking beets and
   horseradish paste)

1 large horseradish

1. The night before, boil beets until soft. Peel and grate. Marinate in 2 cups of the white vinegar. Refrigerate. (Canned beets can be used, but as Papa said, "Let's face it, it just isn't the same.")

2. Peel the horseradish and finely grate in a food processor. Open the windows!

3. Put in bowl. Add enough white vinegar (about ½ cup) to make a horseradish paste.

4. Add ½ cup drained beets per 1 cup horseradish paste. Mix together.

> Yield: Every year there's enough to go around for about 20 guests. Some years less, others more. Papa finds no one is too eager to overdo it on the bitter herbs, but the sweet beets are more popular. If you want to be authentic, leave out the beets! Serve as a garnish for gefilte fish or on the matzoh-*maror* sandwich.

The Remembering

Kwame Alexander

One day next winter
after you've been gone
twenty seasons
and Nandi is looking at an old scrapbook photo
of you lying next to me standing
in Uncle Albert's "especially tailored for"
she'll ask "who was that man sleeping"
and I'll say "is—is that man" "now, grab your shoes and the
    purple jacket"

And then we'll visit 1045 Bells Mill Road
so she can feel the dirt underneath
the house with the big "A" on the front
that you and Granny's thumbless hands built.
And she'll look at her nails and say "ugh, can we go. It's
    chilly"
and I'll remember how, when Albert passed, you gave
    Daddy

his "made in Hong Kong," so I could be warm
"up there near Roanoke with all them cold folks"

Behind your house
we will go walking across the earth's cold floor
past the chicken coop that is no longer there
and I'll stop suddenly and tell her "shhh"
and she'll ask "what are you listenin' for"
and I'll say "listenin' to—dinner"
and with your big eyes she'll look at me strange for a cold
    minute
until I tell her the stories
of how you broke bread with those chickens
fattening them until
Granny cracked their necks and fried their legs
and again she'll say "ugh"

And then I'll show her the new Masonic Lodge
which used to be the old Masonic Hall
which used to be the meeting place for those
angry Negro folks you would hear walking back from church
preaching about taking *us* back to Africa.
And she'll ask "did he go with them"
and I'll smile and rub her head
the way your son used to rub mine
when I made him smile.

And then, when we arrive at your gravesite
down the street from Mount Lebanon Baptist,

I'll jump out the car and open her door
and she'll frown and say "I can do it myself"
and I'll remember watching you
open Granny's door,
even when she told you she could do it herself.

And when we kneel down beside you
to talk of ole times
and pray for new ones
her memory will rekindle
even though she only met you twice
and she will joyfully ask,
as if someone long gone has come home,
"was he my granddaddy too,"
and I'll smile again, my tears frozen in the winter air,
and tell her "is—is my granddaddy"

And then I'll stand up thinking that
I've showed her enough of you
to last us another twenty seasons and
she'll grab my hand real tight
like she's thinking something
and say "I like your coat, Daddy,"
and then I'll pick her up
like you used to do me when I was six
and warmed your heart

Inside the car
we will drive back across the earth's cold floor

back past the church
back past the chickens
back past the house with the big "A" on the front of the house
back to the scrapbook
back to the photo
and while I'm remembering
she'll say "what are you thinking on?"
and I'll say "about—"
thinking about
that strange white-robed man in the picture—
(the one who kept calling you Mr. instead of Deacon)
the one who spoke at your funeral about
how brave and wonderful you were
all the while never mentioning a word
about Marcus Garvey
or Uncle Albert's coat.

Old Silent One

Barbara J. Stevenson

Old Silent One is what I'd say
If I were asked about my grandfather today.
In his blue denim overalls far away
I watched him till the fields all day.
When he finished that task
He'd go to another,
Usually stopping to sup with Grandmother.

As he enters the kitchen
He heads straight for the sink
Disposing of the dirt
Before having a cool drink.
When he sits at the table
He gives honor to God,
Thanks him for his meal
   His life
     And his job.

His hands like claw pliers,
He picks up a biscuit,
Sops it in gravy,
And quick past his whiskers.
The melting sensation is all over his face
As he reaches for another to take its place.

Up from the dinner table,
Back on the job.
He pokes through all kinds of junk that he brought.
Something that looked like a wishbone, I thought.
No, child! Grandpa would say.
This is a plow that I used with a horse one day.

Fading sunlight

               Lightning Bugs

                             Clear, Starry Nights.

Bible in hand

               Reading verse after verse

                       Old Silent One drifts into a peaceful reverie.

Grandfather Story

🎮🎮🎮

The Honorable Dolores H. Fridge

"Charles!" I can still hear the voice of my grandmother calling his name—high-pitched, insistent. He would smile at me, coal-black eyes, smooth dark skin, with cheekbones that sat high on his face, black wavy hair, and a raspy but gentle voice.

"Golden," he would say back to my grandmother, "I'm only giving the girl a little coffee and a lot of cream." He would wink at me, his favorite granddaughter, and pour half a cup of dark, rich, stove-brewed coffee. The cream ran almost as rich, and I loved the combination. It was one of my favorite moments—coffee and cream with Granddaddy Charles.

We sat across the table from each other. Beside us was a window which panoramaed the West Virginia hills and the railroad tracks that carried coal from the mines of "Number 9." He pointed out things, told stories, and answered my endless streams of questions. I was a curious and very verbal child. I can remember the glistening black eyes, which al-

CHARLES STARLING

ways smiled on me with favor. This man, who I now realize was small in stature and thin, was a giant to me. It is strange, for I can't remember much about the stories he told me, but as I write this, the essence of who my grandfather Charles was comes back to me.

His presence made me feel safe—his voice and manner of speech were both comforting and endearing. He called me Fruppie and smiled and poured more rich coffee and cream into my cup. He asked about me and what I had been doing—I responded eagerly and with great detail and reveled in the attention and his tenderness. My grandmother was across the kitchen, making biscuits and bacon on the coal stove. Occasionally I would hear her chuckle at our conversation, and every now and then she would say "Charles"—in that way that only she could do—and he would smile at me and pour more coffee and cream and we would talk on.

When we moved to Cleveland and went back to visit in West Virginia, I waited for the first morning back, because I knew it would be coffee and cream, by the window looking out at the hillside: trains carrying coal, moving back and forth, and Granddaddy Charles—gentle, kind, patient, adoring his youngest granddaughter, and in the process teaching her how to love. Teaching her what to expect, at least what to look and hope for.

He never yelled or accused. When I did "dumb" things, he would question "Why?" and somehow, when my response was shared and his wisdom imparted, I knew what to do, or not to do, the next time, yet my sense of self was never tainted by the experience. I never felt "dumb" or that he loved me less. I simply knew what to do if there was a next time.

I always knew that I was loved by this man for who I was, and that was good. It has helped me stay whole through some of the worst times. I miss him.

BUT IT STOPPED . . . SHORT

For John and Norman

Shannon M. Cotter

i still see him
racing me down our fishing pier
unfettered by the crutch at his side

i still hear him
weaving me into his fairy tales
and teaching me irish lullabies

i still feel him
his giant callused hands
cuddling me tight
and his week-old jack-o'-lantern lips
kissing me good night

and i recognize
of the men i have known

and those i am bound to meet
inevitably not one will make me feel
as lovely powerful or complete
as the men i have called
grandfather

A Toast to Bill

Eugenia Collier

Sometimes life blesses us with rare and wonderful gifts. My blessing is to have attained an age at which I can reach back in memory as far as my great-grandmother, born black in a slave state over a century ago, and forward to my two tiny great-grandchildren, whose future world of technology and multiracialism I cannot envision.

I string the generations together like precious pearls, one atop another. I am the middle pearl, observer of all. I can say to the ancestors, "I have been where you have been," and to the descendants, "I have been where you will go." For we all share the same ultimate journey, although the terrain may vary.

Looking back at those who created me, I note the happy irony that the most interesting of my ancestors was not even related to me by blood. Bill Lewis. Grandma's second husband, he was not the biological father of her children. But he was the only father they knew, and to us he was Granddaddy. In Grandma's house he was always an outsider, probably by choice. In a house of teetotalers, he liked his little nip every now and then. This essay is my toast to my grandfather Bill.

My dad was a floor-baby when his own father died; my uncle Nelson was a lap-baby; and the two girls were little older than toddlers. Bill had loved my grandma Minnie when they were very young in old Baltimore. But Bill was rough-hewn—not "refined" and light-skinned, as her sisters preferred. (Old Baltimore was strictly segregated racially, then segregated again as the oppressed divided ourselves into light and dark, affluent and impoverished, professional and working-class.) Besides, Bill belonged to a world that they rejected: He was a railroad man, a cook on the B & O. He drank with his cronies, cussed when somebody made him mad, lived life as he chose, and took no mess off of anybody.

Minnie was slender and beautiful, with clear hazel eyes and long light hair tumbling over her shoulders. She was soft but strong, like silk. Maybe she just wasn't ready for a man like Bill. She married a handsome youth who was, they say, half Irish. He was in some ways the opposite of Bill Lewis: a gentle person who wrote poetry, they tell me, he loved books. He worked for the Post Office and died of pneumonia as a young man. Left a widow with four tiny children at a time when black women were at the bottom of the economic ladder, Minnie turned to her family. She moved in with one of her sisters, and the family survived. Their brother Harry struggled to establish an insurance company, which gave his sisters jobs.

Bill Lewis came courting again—but this time he had to include not only Minnie's four sisters but also her four children. Decades later, he recalled how, on a Sunday afternoon, he rented a horse and buggy to take his Minnie for a drive, but he had to take various and sundry of her relatives, too. The poor horse struggled along the cobblestone streets until he got to a steep hill on St. Mary's Street; try as he might, he could *not* pull all those people up that hill. So they all had to get out, in their Sunday finery, and trudge up the hill after the relieved horse.

Bill and Minnie married. They lived together peacefully all their lives. Probably they made many compromises of which I will never know. Her children always called him Mr. Lewis. I wonder now whether this was an acknowledgment that he was never quite family: husband but not father. For, even in this crowded household, he was essentially alone. In all his tales of his past, he only once mentioned parents or siblings. No relatives ever visited. He had no former wife or any children of his own. The house and the household were Minnie's. But every now and then he would have a jolly evening with one or another of his cronies in the basement kitchen, where he was king.

Bill was Virginia-born in the first generation after slavery. All his life, he bore a scar on his head from an injury that had occurred in his infancy: his mother, clambering down a ladder in an escape from slavery, dropped her baby son. She had been held in bondage even though legal slavery had ended a generation earlier.

The kitchen was the hub of the household. It encompassed more than half of the basement, which ran the whole length and width of that massive house. There were three rooms in the basement. At the bottom of the stairs was a dark, spooky room with one small window, beneath which lay a mountain of coal. The room was dominated by a monstrous furnace, its roar muted by a heavy iron door. The dogs and cats went into that dark room to give birth. To me, in my earliest years, the room was populated by unspeakable things; I skittered fearfully past its shut door. On the side of the basement was a larger room with a round table and a number of wooden chairs. Here we ate most of our meals, while our neighbors strolled past the basement windows, only their feet and legs visible. The eating room opened into the kitchen—the underground domain that nurtured the household.

Bill Lewis' kingdom. There he sat in a lavishly carved wooden rocking chair, painted green. Bill—the king on his throne, giving directions when cooking was happening, and weaving tales about his glory days on the railroad and his adventures in old Baltimore. Often he was sipping beer. We would all be there, the surrogate family that Grandma had assembled: James and Virginia, a boy and girl who lived with us and did the chores; my cousin Catty, a white child whom my aunt Fiddy had adopted (she and Aunt Fiddy lived on the third floor when Aunt Fiddy was between husbands); Mr. Lipscomb, who dropped in daily and did heavier chores; Paul Lawson, a housepainter who also dropped by daily, in case we had a house to be painted; a person whom we called Crazy Bill, whose function remains unclear; my brother, Maceo; and sundry dogs and cats. And me, the youngest.

I was an isolated, withdrawn child with virtually no self-esteem, only the basic instinct for survival that makes the lowest creature flee from the predator. "You are an *unnatural* child," my mother told me angrily when I was about four. "You never kiss your father like other little girls." I was hurt and puzzled: I did not know that little girls were supposed to kiss their fathers. Certainly nobody was kissing me. Or touching me at all.

The one place I felt at ease was in Granddaddy's kitchen. We were a separate world, there in the depths of the house. People came and went—mostly through the back door— some to go through the motions of doing chores, but many to sit around and rap and sometimes to eat whatever was on the stove. Bill Lewis dominated it all, sitting on his throne-rocker, gripping a can of beer like a scepter and taking an occasional guzzle. Many a passionate discussion took place in that kitchen—about politics, family members, the world, trivia—but the best talk of all was Bill's reminiscences. He would hold forth on his adventures on the railroad—the times he went drinking with the poet Paul Laurence Dunbar, chatted with the author James Weldon Johnson, got involved in a heated discussion on religion between two passengers, one of whom was Lew Wallace, who went home and wrote *Ben Hur.* He told of hilarious incidents with his buddies, who were now staid old men. I was too young to contribute anything to the discussions, but I loved being part of the group, completely accepted. I sat on a stool next to Bill's chair. He was the center of warmth which radiated through the whole large room. Perhaps the magic was the fact of our individual aloneness; each of us was "making it" without much (or any) support from family. But in Bill's kitchen, we communicated with each other on a level of which none of us was aware.

As I write this essay, more than sixty-five years melt away, I am back in Granddaddy's kitchen. The babble of voices, punctuated by James' loud, wonderful laugh; the aroma of stew or applesauce or something indefinable on the stove; the warmth of a fat puppy on my lap; the assortment of people of various ages, from my brother and me to Granddaddy and Mr. Lipscomb; of various colors, from white Catty to dark James; of different pasts and different futures—they all return to me in memory with a vividness surprising after so many years. We were, to me, a family, and Bill Lewis was the magnet that drew us all together.

On one unforgettable occasion, Granddaddy made us all inexpressibly proud. When I was ten, the Elks, a secret benevolent society, had a grand parade, which swept down Madison Avenue, past our house, with banners, fabulous costumes, marching bands whose strut was enough to send a sinner to Jesus! Yes, my Lord! All these decades later, I thrill to the boom-boom-boom of the drums, I see the high-stepping marchers and the drum majors gone crazy, and my spirit rises from this chair and marches with them, as I wanted to do then. At the climax of the parade was an open car. And there in the backseat was Granddaddy, arrayed in top hat and tails! And right there in front of all that crowd, *he grinned at us and waved!* It was a proud moment. He *waved!*

I sensed then that Granddaddy was a very important dignitary in the Elks, but many years passed before I knew his real significance. The Benevolent and Protective Order of the Elks, a national fraternity, was strictly segregated. Blacks were not permitted to join the whites in their benevolence and protection. As a railroad man, Bill Lewis spent a lot of time in Cincinnati, where he joined a black Elks lodge. When he settled in Baltimore, he took the lead in founding a fraternity for black people, which they called the Improved Benevolent and Protective Order of the Elks. My granddaddy was highly honored. I remember a huge stuffed elk's head in our hallway—we used to hang Christmas lights on it. Other black lodges in Baltimore were ultimately founded. Bill Lewis' lodge, Monumental Lodge #3, is still active and going strong.

Sometime after we started school, Granddaddy would take Maceo, Minna, and me to the movies on Friday nights. Minna was Uncle Nelson's daughter; they lived in the next block up the street, for black families lived close together in those days of segregation. Minna was my best friend. Granddaddy would gather us into his car, and we would go chugging down Pennsylvania Avenue.

The Avenue in those days wasn't the cesspool of crime and desperation that it has become. Forbidden access to downtown Baltimore by custom and by law, the black community created its own "downtown." On the Avenue we had theaters, shops, cabarets, a market, an eating place or two. And an unmistakable air of blackness—an air of festivity, a feeling of joy after labor and travail. The Avenue was big on the black entertainment circuit. Billie, the Duke, Ella, the Ink Spots—the greatest black entertainers performed on the stage of the Royal Theater. The Avenue was lit up and lively.

The years passed and, as years do, they wrought many changes. After college I married; being young and absolutely broke, we moved into an apartment on the third floor of my parents' house. Before long, in quick succession, we had two tiny boys.

In her mid-seventies, Grandma broke her hip a second time, and she didn't recover. For a while Granddaddy wandered around the empty house like a body without a soul. Then my parents brought him to live out his years with us.

Granddaddy's old spirit was gone. At first he would spend his time with us in the den, intrigued by the new toy, television. Sometimes he would sit in front of the TV alone, ostensibly watching, but the picture would have gone awry and would be a distortion of lights and shadows and strange shapes. We knew then that he was going blind. He talked a lot to Maceo, telling him about life in the old days. He spent more and more time alone in his room, a large back room a bit apart from the other bedrooms. We all dropped in several times a day. He would be sitting in his rocking chair, his sole possession from the old home, napping or sightlessly gazing at the wall. He still enjoyed his beer. He found willing beer-runners in my little fellows. He would say to one of my babies, "Go get me little beer." And my angel-child would toddle downstairs to the refrigerator. Before they were three, my little ones knew the difference between a can of beer and a can of soda. For a little while, in the comfortable glow of beer, Granddaddy would be the old Bill, reared back on his throne, king of his world.

It was then that I started calling him Bill. I don't remember why—perhaps because there was nobody left to call him that. He began calling me Dearie and sometimes Dear Heart. As Christmas approached, I tried to make fruitcakes and eggnog under his direction, but the project was a dismal failure. I was a recipe-cook, and he was an instinct-cook. He needed to see and to touch as he cooked. The fruitcakes were flat and tasteless; the eggnog was a watery white mess that tasted like insect spray. The old days were gone forever.

Bill decayed rapidly. My mother tended him faithfully through all the nastiness of prolonged dying. He told her once that every morning when he awoke he was disappointed, because he had hoped to die in his sleep. Finally, he got his wish.

My grandfather Bill was not a storybook grandfather. As a child, I never sat on his lap and absorbed any words of wisdom. We never walked hand in hand through gardens while he explained the workings of the universe. He never even favored me above his other grandchildren. But he meant more to me than either of us knew. In my miserable early years, his kitchen was for me a place of security and joy. He loved me for myself, just as I was. Perhaps he sensed in me the same spirit that had enabled him to rise from his birth in illegal bondage to mastery of his life. He made hard choices and lived with them. He had the wisdom and the strength to compromise, yet he lived his life with flair and permitted nobody to define him. His example, rather than his words, showed the way to any who would see.

I am older now than he was when I sat at his feet listening to his stories. The years have taught me who he was and what he meant to me. I reach out to him across time and dimension. And I offer a toast to my grandfather, not in drinks but in words.

Here's to you, Bill—with love and gratitude.

The Warm Hearth Writers' Workshop

About six months before one of the great hearts of the modern world decided to beat a different rhythm for the angels, Alex Haley visited Warm Hearth Writers' Workshop in Blacksburg, Virginia. He was tired that morning, but as he started to speak to us he rose from his chair, turned it around, and leaned on it much as one would lean on a back fence. Alex always loved to talk, and this morning the more he shared, the more energy he seemed to be taking in. He was talking to a workshop in which the youngest member was about seventy-five and the oldest was ninety-eight. Alex was always a lover of ancestors and he was reminding Warm Hearth that they must continue to tell their stories so that one day great-grandchildren, just like himself, could share a Pulitzer Prize–winning story like *Roots*.

I have had the pleasure of working with Warm Hearth for nine years. We are a retirement community but our retirement is from a salaried job, not a vital life. Warm Hearth ancestral stories go back into the middle of the last century, the nineteenth century; go back before the Civil War; go through the changes of this great century of ours, the twentieth—leaving tracks through the emotional wilderness that says humans can and must triumph over fear and violence. Warm Hearth stories say we have survived and with love others like us will continue too.

The following six entries were written by members of the Warm Hearth Writers' Workshop.

—Nikki Giovanni

Great-Grandfather Levi Goodell

Vivian E. Timmerman

My great-grandfather Levi Goodell was born June 22, 1840, at Ellisville, Fulton County, Illinois, to Samuel and Sarah Bronson Goodell, the last of eleven children. In 1861, at the age of twenty-one, he enlisted in Company D, 55th Illinois Volunteer Infantry, as a private, to serve in the Civil War for three years. At the end of those three years, he re-enlisted for three more as a veteran volunteer. He was mustered out with his company August 14, 1865, as a sergeant at the end of the war.

He fought in the battles of Shiloh, Chattanooga, and Chickamauga, and was on Sherman's March to the Sea. He suffered severe pains for ten days from the near passage of a shell that so stunned him he fell to the ground during the Battle of Shiloh. Those pains were to bother him again as he grew older. At the close of the war, he was honored to be chosen to participate in the Grand Review at Washington, D.C.

In 1996, an old trunk stored in the attic of one of Levi's relatives was opened and found to contain packs of time-worn, faded letters written to and from a special girlfriend named Sarah Ann Fielding, whom he left behind when he joined the Army.

Grandfather brought home an old pieced quilt when he returned. There are several conflicting stories as to how he got the quilt, so no one knows what the truth is. Because each of his four granddaughters wanted the quilt after he died, it was cut in fourths, and each has a part of it. The piece I saw had been beautifully framed and hung on a bedroom wall by his great-grandson.

There was much rejoicing among his entire family and especially by that special girl, Sarah Ann, when Levi returned after four years of a war in which brother was pitted against brother. There were members of the Goodell family fighting on both sides.

Sarah and Levi were married December 31, 1865, in Prairie City, Illinois. Shortly afterward, the Levi Goodells began their pioneer life northwest of Cuba, Illinois, in a place called Buckeye. Levi hauled logs to a nearby mill, picked up the lumber, and built a one-room frame house for his bride. After three years of very hard work building and beautifully furnishing the one-room house, they sold it, loaded their goods in a horse-drawn wagon, and departed for Mansfield, Illinois. There they bought eighty acres of land west of town for a total of two hundred dollars.

Levi again hauled lumber, from a mill sixteen miles away, and built another one-room house, to which he added a kitchen after three years. All six of their children were born there. Later, three bedrooms, a front for the house, and a barn were added.

Sarah and Levi were devout Christians and always found a church to attend and serve wherever they lived. Their daughters were trained to be Sunday-school teachers by Sarah.

After thirty-one years in this location, they sold their land for ninety dollars an acre, which was considered a very good price, and moved to Humboldt, Iowa, to buy 167 acres of equally good land at thirty-seven dollars an acre. The land boom was still on, and young farmers were advised to "go west, go west, young man"; many of them did.

At the age of seventy, in 1910, Levi was having back problems. His family was grown, so he sold half his acres to his oldest son, kept the other half for rental property, and bought an eight-room house in Humboldt. What a castle that house was, after they had lived as pioneers for so long. During the next thirteen years, Levi was active in civic and church work—mostly as a volunteer, but he did some paid city jobs.

It was during these years that I was old enough to know and enjoy my great-grandfather. He would sit with my sisters and me on the doorstep of our house, sing songs, and tell us stories. We especially liked the Civil War songs his comrades used to sing, and the stories about his childhood, when he didn't have all the advantages we were having.

Levi was a wonderful, influential, loving, devout, and caring father, grandfather, and great-grandfather. It is indeed a privilege to have known and to remember him. His influence is felt far and wide through the many descendants he has left.

My Civil War Grandfather

Margaret Worley

I never knew my grandfather Joseph Umbarger, because he died when I was about six months old. But I heard so many interesting stories about him when I was growing up, especially about his years in the Civil War, that he became a real presence in my life.

According to Goodrich's book *Smyth County: History of Traditions,* by 1860 "rumblings of Civil War" possibility reached Marion, Virginia. Six squads of patrols were formed to keep order in the county if problems developed.

Joe Umbarger joined one of the squads as a private in April 1861—the first company from Smyth County. He was twenty-seven years old at the time, and fought in the ill-fated Pickett's Charge.

On the third day of the Battle of Gettysburg, he was wounded and had to drop back from the fighting.

Years later, he described what had happened to his remaining child, Annie Laura (my mother): "On the third day of the siege of Gettysburg, the shells were coming thick and fast. All at once I felt a pain in my left arm; then it fell to my side, blood covered my hand, and the pain was unbearable. I had to drop back. I made a tourniquet and fastened it above the wound. Then I started walking toward the nearest hospital. I stopped at every stream to rest and wash my wound. Finally, I reached a makeshift hospital. A doctor examined my arm and told me the maggots had kept it from becoming infected. When I healed sufficiently, I gratefully returned to my family."

Joe's arm was amputated on July 3, 1863. He was discharged from the army on January 2, 1865. He lived with his family on their farm near Marion and did all he could to help.

Joe married Nancy Margaret Fudge on August 8, 1878, when he was forty-five years old and she was forty-two. He took Margaret to the old home place where he lived with his family. They adjusted and enjoyed their lives. Their first child, a son, died at birth. Annie Laura, their second and last child, was born at home on December 11, 1880.

Joe and Margaret provided a happy home for their daughter. There were no schools near them, but Joe wanted his daughter to get an education. He located a school several miles away, and found a family who was willing to have her live with them so she could attend the school. Each Monday morning he drove her to their house, and returned to get her on Friday afternoons. She completed what we call high school today.

Joe was determined to get her to college, and she decided to go to Martha Washington (women only) in Abingdon,

Virginia, so Joe drove her to Marion to catch the train to Abingdon. After her third year, Joe became ill and she felt she must stay home and care for him.

Annie Laura met a good-looking young man, brother of a college friend. After several months of courtship, they were married, and her husband, Carl, moved in with Joe and Margaret and took over the responsibility of caring for the farm.

In August 1909, Joe's first granddaughter was born. He and Margaret spent many hours enjoying the new baby. But then Joe's health became much worse, and on January 17, 1910, at age seventy-seven, he died. Three months later, Margaret followed him.

My Grandfather

Gertrude Weissenborn

My paternal grandfather died many years before I was born, so I did not know him. In his wedding picture he was a handsome man with curly black hair, a beard, and brown eyes. He came from Germany and homesteaded near Gaylord, Minnesota. He died of tuberculosis at age forty-nine, when my father, the oldest of the living children was only twelve.

My father inherited the farm, and I was born there in 1915.

Grandfather Spiering also came from Germany, with his wife and three children. A brother-in-law had preceded him and lent him money to come to America. By coincidence, they settled on the farm next to Grandfather Abraham. Soon after their arrival, Grandmother Spiering went into labor, and Grandmother Abraham, who was a midwife, delivered her twins. One of the twins was my mother. Grandmother Spiering was not prepared for twins, so Grandmother Abraham went home and sewed extra baby clothes.

At first they were very poor. My mother said the children could not go to church because they had no shoes to wear. Grandfather Spiering fashioned some crude foot protection out of leather for winter. In summer they went barefoot.

Grandfather Spiering homesteaded near Winthrop, Minnesota, the next village. Under the Homestead Act of 1862, "Any person who is the head of a family, or who has arrived at the age of twenty-one years, and is a citizen of the United States, or who shall have filed his declaration to become such," could get 160 acres. He needed only to pay a small filing fee, live there for five years, and make certain improvements. Then he received a free title.

A man of average height and weight, Grandfather always carried himself very erect, perhaps because of his military service in Germany. He was a nice-looking man. When I knew him, he was already gray and had a full gray beard. I thought he looked like the patriarchs in Bible pictures. I never heard him raise his voice or display anger.

Grandma and Grandpa had ten children—seven daughters, three sons. He had come to America to make his fortune, and that was all-important. He did not believe in education. My mother was sent to school just long enough to learn to read and write in German so she could be confirmed, about two years. She went to what they called the German School, which was actually the Lutheran School. Unfortunately, in those days the state didn't compel children to attend school. Grandpa told his family it was more important to make money; the children all had to work hard on the farm.

Years later, when I attended college, my mother said, "An education is something no one can take away from you."

The year before my mother married, Grandpa had a new house built on the farm. Before that, the children often woke up on winter mornings with a covering of snow on their beds.

Grandpa prospered, and each daughter received three thousand dollars when she married. I never heard what the sons received, but it must have been as much if not more: the Germans seemed to favor sons. My mother said she never saw her money, because Grandpa gave it directly to my dad. She was in love with another young man, but he didn't own a farm and Grandpa forbade her to marry him.

When they were in their fifties, the grandparents retired and moved to a nice house on the outskirts of Winthrop. There they had a little acreage and could keep a cow, some chickens, and a couple of cats, raise some corn, grow a big garden and a nice lawn. Grandma had a hernia, so Grandpa did all the heavy work. He could walk to town to get his supplies. For church services, one of their nearby children picked them up.

I can't remember ever being touched or held by either grandparent. When we came to visit, they would look us over and remark how we had grown. Once, when I was about eight, Grandpa commented that I seemed to have a strong chest. I did not see the significance of that, but because it was the only personal remark he ever made about me, it meant something to me.

There were forty-seven grandchildren that I know about, and I believe some who died in infancy. When Grandpa or

Grandma had a birthday, we had a ball. There was a big spread in age levels, so not all grandchildren were ever there at the same time. Besides, two of the children lived too far away to attend. Still, there were enough to make it fun. We went to say hello to Grandpa's cow. We played in his pasture, where the big cattails grew. One boy cousin suggested they would make lovely torches if soaked in oil. Oh no, we could never play with fire! We marched on the wooden walk to the outhouse. That made a lovely sound.

While the mothers cooked a sumptuous meal the men played cards, Grandpa smoking his pipe. When it was time to eat, the men were served at the first table. After that the mothers ate dinner. The children were the last to be served. Sometimes all the best cake was gone by then. Food didn't have a high priority for us that day. The thought of sliding down the hall banister after dinner was much more important.

One evening, driving home after one of our parties, my mother asked, "Did anyone see Grandpa's cats today?" We laughed. The smart cats had gone into hiding as soon as all those children appeared.

Grandpa was seventy-nine when he died. During his final illness, the daughters took turns caring for him in his home. It was customary to bring the body back from the funeral parlor into the home for a family service before the church service. I was one of the grandchildren who were there to clean the house for the service when they brought Grandpa's body back. I was shocked: my grandmother cried bitterly when she saw his casket. I had never seen her cry before.

When the estate was settled, the children again received some money. This time Grandpa couldn't hand it to my dad. My mother took the money and went right out and bought the family a new Chevrolet sedan. She had earned it the old-fashioned way, by working for it.

Ralph Earl Prime

John Murray

Ralph Earl Prime, my maternal grandfather, was born in Matteawan, New York, on March 29, 1840, and died on December 27, 1920. He was the eldest of five children of Alanson Jermain Prime and Ruth Havens Higbie Prime. He was named after his great-grandfather Ralph Earl, the early-American portrait painter. He was admitted to the practice of law in 1861 and spent 1861, 1862, and part of 1863 as a soldier in the Army of the U.S. for the suppression of the Rebellion, enlisting as a private and later nominated by President Lincoln as a brigadier general.

Upon returning from the war, he settled in Yonkers, New York, where he practiced law with his brother in the firm of R. E. and A. J. Prime. On August 9, 1866, he married Sarah Ann Richards in Utica, New York. Sarah's mother had died when Sarah was five years old. Her father, Jacob Richards, a practicing physician, apparently felt incapable of acting as a single parent, so Sarah became a foster daughter of her maternal grandfather, Reverend Calvin Wolcott, and her name was changed to Annie Richards Wolcott. Though her marriage certificate gives her name as Sarah Ann Richards, Ralph preferred to call her Annie.

Ralph and Annie had eight children: four sons and four daughters. My mother, Arabella, was the youngest daughter. Ralph was very active as a layman in the Presbyterian Church, serving as a ruling elder and as moderator of the Synod of New York. He wrote a number of articles on church matters, from a strongly conservative, legalistic point of view. Our family spent summers at Fishers Island with Ralph and Annie. I often went to church at the Union Chapel with Ralph while the rest of the family went to the Episcopal church with Annie. They both had strong views on religion and expected people to stand by their beliefs.

Ralph was active in the Sons of the American Revolution; three of his ancestors had served in that war. He was also active in the corresponding organization for the War of 1812, since one of his grandfathers had served in that war. Ralph traveled widely in Europe and the Orient in 1884, 1888, and 1892. My mother accompanied him on the 1888 trip.

Ralph and Annie delved deeply into genealogy a century ago. They recorded their findings in a printed volume entitled "The Record of My Ancestry," tracing about sixty lines back to the time when they had come to New England in the early seventeenth century.

I was only eleven years old when my grandfather died, in 1920, so I never really knew him intimately. Perhaps I was overawed by his authoritative manner, but my respect for him has grown as I have studied his accomplishments.

Bampy: A Song in the Rain

𝕲𝕲𝕲

Nancy E. Slocum

I don't know why we called him Bampy. Perhaps my oldest cousin, Sally, started it when she lisped out her baby-talk version of "Grandpa." It doesn't matter. Bampy was a very special man, so a unique name fitted him perfectly. I do know that his real name was Albert Morton Thoroman, though I rarely heard it used. His friends called him Mort.

Never in my rather long and eventful life have I known anyone with such an unquenchable spirit, such *joie de vivre,* such encompassing optimism. Bampy has always been the steady beacon of my life. He was an educated historian on a still-raw frontier, one who saw endless promise for the future in the struggles of the past. And of the present.

Born in 1873, Bampy grew up on a dirt farm known then as the Thoroman homestead, in Osage County, Kansas. His parents had made the trek westward from Ohio in a covered wagon shortly before his birth. I know nothing about his early education, whether he gained it at home or in a small frontier school. But he learned enough to enter the University of Kansas at Lawrence, where he graduated in 1909 at age thirty-six. His curiosity about history led to graduate work at K.U. and the University of Chicago, culminating in a Master of Arts degree in U.S. history.

Throughout his higher education, he taught and served as superintendent of several Kansas school systems—providing a slim income for his growing family. He and my grandmother raised four daughters—teachers all, including my mother.

A perennial sparkle dwelt in Bampy's eye, revealing a keen sense of humor behind his restless curiosity. He was interested in everyone and everything. Curious about Europe and eager to help rebuild it after the First World War, he signed on at age forty-six to serve as first secretary of the YMCA in France, and later in Italy. For a few months, he also served with the Educational Corps of the American Expeditionary Forces. His mission accomplished in Europe, and longing for his family, Bampy returned to Kansas and to his work as a school superintendent. He soon became enthusiastically engaged in editing textbooks for the state School Book Commission, and publishing editions of the classics for use in high schools.

At home, Bampy made sure that his daughters extended their experience beyond a parochial, Kansas-centered, view of life. He must have been the first school superintendent in the state to purchase a touring car, and he did it so he could take his family on long cross-country trips to places he considered important for the girls' education. With a cabin tent and poles strapped to the running board, and other camping gear stashed in the trunk, he and Grandmother proceeded to show their daughters all they could of the world. Using the long summer vacations from schoolwork, they toured the dirt roads of the United States and Canada from coast to coast, taking in the capital cities and Eastern Seaboard one summer, and the great national parks of the West the next. They launched an educational tradition that passed down the generations in our family to the present. Having taken my own sons on many an educational long-distance trip, I derive considerable pleasure from seeing my oldest son pack up his brood and camping gear and set off for yet another family adventure. His great-grandfather would have been proud.

For all his educational interests and activities, Bampy was certainly no boring academician. In his great booming voice, he taught us all to sing: campfire songs, nonsense songs, patriotic songs, and hymns. He saw all of history as a great and lurching panorama of progress/backstep/progress in fast-forward, and he told it that way. We, his grandchildren, heard him eagerly, enthralled with his stories of the American frontier. We learned about our country's horrendous treatment of our native peoples, about spectacular feats of railroad-building across a rugged continent, and about our family history of underground railroading long before we were born.

We were fascinated, too, by his riveting descriptions of the desolation wrought by the war in Europe, his indignation at the desecration of the great art treasures of the "Old World," as he called it, and of his hopes that peace would reign now that democracy had been safely installed overseas, or so he thought.

A Republican of the old school, Bampy made us proud to be descended from abolitionist and feminist forebears, and he constantly instilled in us, his numerous granddaughters, the importance of what he called "good citizenship." We knew what he meant, though some of us failed to live up to his challenges. Bampy also believed that our country should never again become entangled in the petty quarrels of Europe. He had seen too much of death and suffering among the wounded and bereaved in the wake of World War I. To him it was unthinkable that another, even worse, war might someday demand our country's youth.

Yet, in the 1930s, as war clouds again darkened distant skies, Bampy became increasingly concerned. And when Bampy worried, we all did. As war spread across Europe, he regularly tuned in his great console radio to the ominous reports from Edward R. Murrow and Eric Sevareid. Bampy gathered us together to huddle over the broadcasts, then to discuss the meaning of what we had just heard.

Bampy's sense of urgency in response to the worsening news had, I now think, a greater impact on us children than I realized at the time. Not only were we growing up in the midst of the worst depression in U.S. history, but my cousins, sister, and I felt keenly—perhaps more so than most American children of the 1930s—the ominous march of Hitler's powerful military machine across a continent Bampy had taught us to love and admire.

Throughout those years, even when my mother lay seriously ill and my father faced unemployment and mounting hospital bills, Bampy remained strong and sure of the ultimate triumph of good over evil. Almost single-handedly, he kept us all from descending into the depths of our own personal depressions. His eye never lost its sparkle, and his gentle teasing kept us all laughing at ourselves even as we learned from him to deal with the tragedies of life. And always we sang—off-key, perhaps, but lustily.

Bampy himself knew about tragedy all too well. His oldest daughter died in the flu epidemic of 1918–19. Another daughter died of breast cancer in 1933, leaving four small children. A third daughter, my mother, died during the Second World War of a postoperative infection, shortly before antibiotics became available for civilians. I can never forget his counsel to me after her death. "Your mother was a remarkable woman," he told me. "Live up to her dreams for you, and remember how she loved to sing when it rained." I remember, too, who taught her to sing.

E. B. House

Elizabeth Spencer

I grew up some nine hundred miles from where my grandfather lived in Fort Collins, Colorado, and got to see him once a year. Every summer my mother would board the Santa Fe train in Oklahoma City and take my two brothers and me to visit grandparents, first her parents in Denver, then my father's parents for a special day or two. Although distant, I always had a love in my heart for this grandfather, whom we children knew as Papa Daddy.

Edward Bishop House came into this world on February 29, 1872, in Evans, Colorado. His parents, Edward Penn House and Charity Bishop House, had migrated to the High Plains country at the foot of the Rocky Mountains four years before from the town of Penn Yan, New York, where his father had been a telegraph operator and lock tender on the Erie Canal. In 1880, the House family moved to Greeley, the Colorado colony and town named after Horace Greeley of "Go west, young man" fame. There were few roads and fewer financial means in this high desert. Nonetheless, opportu-

E. B. HOUSE

nity beckoned amid sagebrush and cactus, with snow-capped mountains looming to the west. My father's biography of his father reads as follows:

Imagine, if you can, a large hay rack hitched to a pair of mules piled high with furniture and household goods. The bed mattresses were put on top of the load and the family rode on top of the mattresses, all but "old Bossy" the milk cow. She was tied on behind making the four mile overland trip afoot.

My grandfather was eight years old at the time, and it was on that trek that young Ed caught his father's dream of making the arid land become fertile farm country. As a man Ed did, in fact, help to make his father's dream become a reality, through civil and irrigation engineering.

The family settled into Greeley. Here Ed and his younger brother, George, grew up and were well known for their boyish pranks. Ed married Harriet Chandler in 1898, and my father was born in 1899, then a daughter, Peg, and a second son, Joe. When my dad was six, his father joined the engineering faculty at the college in Fort Collins, where, as a professor and later dean of engineering, he became known as E.B.

My dad helped his father make the brown cement blocks for their home. When they had finished laying them for the house and one-car garage, E.B. found himself exactly one block short. He was heard to remark later, "If a student of mine had miscalculated by *that* much, I'd have flunked him!"

The garage was built with a narrow pit in the middle so E.B. could get underneath his car to change the oil and make repairs. One day Peg, who had just learned to drive, put the car in the garage only to have one of the front wheels slide off into the pit. Frantic, she finally got a plank under the wheel, with help from her brothers, and was able to back the car safely out. So Father never knew what had happened. She was especially delighted when Father did exactly the same thing one week later.

My dad wrote that his father was a "dynamic disciplinarian" who required strict obedience from his children "as long as we were dependent on him for bed and board." At the same time, his father had a well-developed sense of humor and a sympathetic understanding. "Our father loved young people and there was practically no generation gap between him and his students and children."

I can bear witness to the truth of these words. My grandparents came to visit in Oklahoma when I was fourteen and struggling with cube roots. Papa Daddy sat down with me and carefully explained the procedure, step by step so that I understood, and thus revealed to his granddaughter his gift for teaching.

E.B. was known for his storytelling, and one story became famous at what is now known as Colorado State University. He had driven up into the Rockies alone to fish. He was good at fly-fishing for rainbow trout and that evening was chopping kindling for a fire, intending to fry his catch for supper. His ax slipped and almost completely severed a big toe. What to do? It was getting dark, and the mountain roads were rocky and narrow, without benefit of guard rails, and full of hairpin curves where he would have to back up the car to make the turns.

Then he remembered that he had a needle and thread, and he made up his mind. He took that needle and stitched up his own toe. And when I knew him, he was still walking around with all ten toes.

As a young man, E.B. loved to race bicycles, the kind with a huge front wheel and a tiny rear wheel. To mount the bike you had to have someone hold it for you; then away you would go. I was greatly impressed when I learned that the large silver coffee urn in his dining room was a prize he had won in a bicycle race.

Not all of Grandfather's years were full of accomplishments or happiness. His younger son, Joe, died of typhoid fever at the age of eighteen; E.B. and his wife never quite recovered from the loss. In later years, E.B. became contentious and moody, which was not conducive to peace or tranquillity, either at home or on the college campus.

Nonetheless, in the history compiled for the CSU centennial, E.B. is featured; there is a picture of him at his desk, and a paragraph on the toe story describing him as "flamboyant." What a grandfather.

NEVER TO GO AGAIN

A Man of High Mentality

Christopher Whaley

Every little boy has a hero. From Superman to Batman, Mr. T to Michael Jordan, as little boys growing up we've worshipped them all and done everything from lifting weights to eating our Wheaties so that we could one day grow up and be like Mike! I should know, because I too had my share of heroes, but this one particular hero of mine doesn't slam-dunk a basketball or beat up the bad guys. He's a short, stocky man with curly hair who loves his cattle ranch and pork chops. This brand of hero shoots the breeze with his family and talks back to the television whenever Jeff Bagwell strikes out at the plate. This hero I speak of is my grandfather Clemett Holley.

For as long as I live, I will never forget that rainy night in the summer of 1986. It was my younger brother Brian's sixth birthday, and we were both happy. Earlier that day, we had worn our grandmother down as we rode all over Houston looking for a Rambo rocket-launcher water gun. After visiting three toy stores, we eventually found it, along

with an M-16 water gun and all sorts of Rambo dolls, ban-
dannas, and other plastic toys to play with. After all,
Rambomania was taking the country by storm, and we were
ready to soak our friends with our high-tech water gear.

At eleven years of age, I was a Sylvester Stallone fanatic
and wanted to be Rambo. I spent days fantasizing about
being a gung-ho military hero and saving the country from
the enemy. It was at this time that I learned from my mother
that my grandfather had served his country in World War II
and the Korean War. Paw Paw, as we called him, was not
only a military veteran; he was a hero.

It was Friday night, and with our bellies full of Maw
Maw's salmon fishcakes and French-fried potatoes, Brian
and I waited and waited for Paw Paw to come home from
work. Paw Paw had a Friday-night ritual in which he would
come home from work, kiss Maw Maw (aw, sooky-sooky,
now!), eat, and watch television. However, on this particular
evening it rained very hard, and I started to worry. Maw
Maw assured me that he would be home, just a little late.
Finally, after we had waited for what seemed forever, it was
time for me and Brian to go to bed. Like the little kids we
were, we didn't go to bed right away; there was a television
in our room, and we watched music videos. About an hour
later, we heard the front door open and the sound of a lunch-
box pound the kitchen table. Paw Paw had come home.

Brian and I made a dash for the kitchen. We saw Paw Paw
taking off his shirt and his work boots, an everyday custom.
As always, we shook hands and cracked a few jokes while
Brian danced around the living room like the happy birth-

day boy he was. I told Brian to get his toys, and he returned with his arsenal of water guns and Rambo dolls. When Paw Paw saw the rocket launcher and the M-16, his eyes widened with amazement. As he stood there holding the toy weapons, it dawned on me that the man I called Paw Paw was a military veteran, a hero.

"Hey there, Brianey, that sure is a nice gun you got there," he said with a grin. Then he began to tell us of his days fighting in the Korean War and how he had won battle stars and a bronze star for saving a few lives. I was in awe of Paw Paw as he told story after story about the war and his experiences in a foxhole and the packaged meals he and his fellow soldiers ate. Brian and I laughed as Paw Paw took the M-16 water gun and pretended he was in combat, taking a mock stance right there in the kitchen. Then Paw Paw quietly handed the gun back to Brian and said he had something to show us.

"What is it, Paw Paw?" I asked.

"Oh yeah, Smitney . . . I got something to show you," he said as he pulled a large bag from the closet and held it in front of me and Brian. Paw Paw slowly opened the contents of the bag and revealed a bullet-riddled combat helmet. Brian and I jumped back in horror.

"What's that, Paw Paw?"

"Smitney, it's a helmet I pulled off a soldier in the war. I brought it home as a souvenir," he said with a grin.

Brian and I stood side by side in shock. Paw Paw explained to us that he had taken the helmet from a fallen soldier as a souvenir of the Korean War. After gazing at the helmet for a while, I finally took it from him and studied the shape, the texture, and the look of history. I placed the helmet on my head and felt like a soldier, ready to defend my country. I felt proud to be the grandson of a man who had sacrificed years of his life to uphold democracy and many of the rights that we have today. For the moment, Rambo didn't matter to me anymore; Paw Paw was the real hero. Needless to say, after the horror story Paw Paw told us about how he got the helmet, Brian and I didn't sleep that night!

My freshman year in high school, I became a member of the Naval Junior Reserve Officers Training Corp. When I donned my service dress uniform for the first time, it was one of the proudest moments in my life. When Paw Paw saw me in uniform, he stood before me and offered me a military salute. He called me a "man of high mentality"; I was not only overwhelmed, but honored. I felt as if I had been recognized by royalty, to have my grandfather, my hero, acknowledge my achievements. Throughout my high-school career, I would receive many honors and accolades for my achievements in NJROTC, including recognition from former President George Bush and the former chairman of the Joint Chiefs of Staff, General Colin Powell. Each and every time I was awarded a medal, a ribbon, or a shoulder cord, I thought about how proud my hero was of me and how proud I was of my hero.

Whenever I hear the national anthem or see an American flag, I salute out of respect for my country and I salute for my grandfather. It is because of Paw Paw that I have the right to liberties I wouldn't have had years ago. Not only do

I salute my Paw Paw, but I give respect and I tip my hat to all grandfathers who gave their time and their lives so that young men like my brother, Brian, and I can achieve anything we set our minds to do. As I said, as little boys we all have our heroes. However, not everyone can meet Michael Jordan or talk to Evander Holyfield, but when your hero is your grandfather he is always part of your life.

209 Tanyard Road

John Noelle Moore

Mr. Tip,
Tipton Hughes Hudson,
Papa to me, my grandfather.

Papa,
youngest of twelve,
who left Hargrave Military Academy
to come home
and care for his aging father and mother,
Mr. Charlie and Miss Fannie,
in the brick house at 209 Tanyard Road,
just outside the town limits of Rocky Mount,
the county seat of Franklin.

Papa,
whose garden grew
tall corn yellow and white,
limas and squash and peas,

tomatoes and cucumbers, and, of course,
the long snap beans,
Irish potatoes and sweet potatoes,
his garden bordered by
an arbor of Concord grapes
and my grandmother Mildred's marigolds.

Papa,
who put wheat in the wheat house,
and corn in the crib,
who hung hams in the smokehouse,
and stacked wood in the woodhouse
for the Warm Morning reigning
in the kitchen, where Mildred
stoked the stove and cooked and warmed
the blue-tiled world
with her gentle grace.

Papa,
who owned two tractors,
the green John Deeres,
the A and the B,
who pulled the hay wagon
to the old Siller Place behind Bald Knob
and bailed the hay and stacked it high
in the barn that stared across Tanyard Road
at the face of Papa's house;
who failed to trim the boxwoods
that outgrew the lane

leading to the front porch
and became a leafy fortress for
the first three grandsons,
my older brother Jesse and me,
and our cousin Charles.

Papa,
whose anger spoke in silence,
whose hand was rarely raised.
Papa, who would let go,
the peacemaker.

Papa,
dark and handsome
in the Hargrave photo, the military man,
his eyes looking somewhere
beyond the silver frame encircling him
in my aunt Emily's library.

Papa,
who wore a Stetson on Sunday
and smoked a pipe,
who sang "Amazing Grace"
in the Furnace Creek Baptist Church choir,
who held in deep baritone
the last note of every hymn,
his vibrato dancing in the silence
of the other singers.

Papa,
who drove his blue Dodge pickup
uptown and downtown
at twenty-five miles an hour,
who stopped for coffee
each morning at The Hub.
Who drove his car on the West Virginia Turnpike,
forced by the law to exceed
his normal speed,
his compliance cheered
by my adolescent brother's laughter
and my grandmother's smile
reflected in the little square mirror
on the turned-down sun visor
as they sped
toward Matewan and our Aunt Did.

Papa,
who drove the lawnmower
in his last years
round and round the ample yard
and into The Bottom,
the green field in front of the house,
the companion
to the front yard's maples and poplars,
to the white latticework wellhouse
and the brown concrete walks,
the paths of decades of feet
on their way to our back door.

Papa,
who told me one autumn afternoon
as we drove to the Roanoke hospital
to visit my grandmother,
"Your mammy's sick in the worst way";
Papa, who could not say
"cancer" and said
no more.

Papa,
who one day reclined too far
on his riding mower,
reclined and could not right himself,
a synapse snapped.

Papa,
who finally curled up
in the position of the nearly born
and stopped.
Stopped,
despite my aunt Martha Ann's giggly
"Now, look at Papa. Looking at those pretty
Miss America girls on TV. . . . Aren't you, Daddy?"

Papa,
who did not see any girls,
who stared into the darkness
of the blankest blank.

Papa,
whose walnut bed disappeared
into a chrome-and-white rental,
Papa rolled up and Papa rolled down,
until
one Sunday afternoon in a hot July
he sighed
deeply
while his four daughters ringed his bed round
and my mother, the eldest, sat out
on the front porch, staring across The Bottom
at the National Guard Armory.

Papa,
who stared
in minutes so long that
my cousin's wife, a licensed practical nurse,
pulled the shades on his failed light.

And in that summer heat
no one moved.
It was the long-awaited, never-expected
ending that none of the daughters
could begin.

Papa speechless and
they speechless, immobile,
en tableau,
girls again.

"Goodbye, Mr. Tip,"
the black man who worked beside
Papa in the fields would say
the next day, doffing his hat.
"Now, that Mr. Tip,
He sho' was some some-kinda-man."

WHEN THE OLD MAN DIED

Wicker Rocking Chair

Thomas W. Giovanni

When I hear people talk about my grandfather, I feel like the last one to look up after a shooting star has burned away. Everyone's oohing and smiling, and there I am, clueless, asking, "What'd I miss?" I know my grandfather far more from the effects he left than directly.

I guess the meteorite image is less than accurate, even if it is my true feeling. He died when I was twelve, and I didn't live with him regularly until I was ten. He and my grandmother lived in Cincinnati, and before we moved there, my mother and I would come from New York to visit in the summer and Christmas. But I did know my grandfather for a while, and he did teach me before he left. He and his chair showed me a few important things.

My grandfather had a rocking chair—wicker, with a cushion as big as I was when I remember seeing it first, at six or so. It stayed at the kitchen table, like another person in the house. In my mind, that chair had existed forever before I met it, a fixture of the world. Just like he did. It and he were like trees or math, telling time or wearing pants: things a child learns are the way they are for no particular reason other than that they are, no matter what crazed explanation adults offer. I suppose I knew better even then, but it was my silent belief that he really lived in that chair. He was there most nights when I went to bed, just rocking. He was in that chair before I woke, up, rocking and drinking coffee. From that chair, he showed me things; he taught me.

He showed me a man—the last adult male I will see at home until I'm looking in the mirror, worrying about my own (as yet unborn, but harassing me already) insane children. He did man things from that chair, like it was his base of operations or something. From his post, he'd look out at the backyard and declare, "That yard needs trimming," or "Those bushes are getting too thick." But there's more to tell about the bushes later. The chair was strategically placed so that he could also see a corner of the front door. He didn't say "Who goes there!" but in all other ways he acted like a sentry, or a lazy guard dog, leaning forward in the chair to see and interrogate. He rarely went to the door himself when anyone else was home, but he often did the majority of talking to whoever showed up. He'd take in the news of the neighborhood from his perch. Leaning forward, he'd listen. He'd smile when someone brought him good news, like who had a baby, or who just graduated. He'd "frown up" (one of his favorite terms) at the sad news. Then, rocking back, he'd issue his proclamations: "That's so nice to hear," or "I knew that boy was no good when I first saw him." He was a good listener, from what I saw, but I also saw that he rarely let information change his mind after a certain point; he merely sifted through a story to glean what would bolster his feeling. I have imitated that resoluteness (obstinacy) also, and the ability to take in information yet not be swayed easily has so far served me well in law school, where one's actual opinion is irrelevant so long as the position adopted is argued well. Professors and judges write on and on, throwing words at me, but I see my grandfather in his chair, and my mind is made up.

Occasionally, when he wasn't in it, I'd jump into the chair and swing my feet back and forth. I say he wasn't in the chair, but I really don't mean that. He smoked cigars, cigarettes, and—this is a positive only to male preadolescents—he wasn't shy about passing gas. So he was *never out* of the chair, even if he wasn't sitting in it. I would sit in the chair and look out into the yard, and I'd say to myself, "That yard needs a little dodgeball." If people came to the door, I'd check 'em out from the guardhouse. Trying to lean far enough forward, I'd almost tip over, but I was ready to give the interrogation, if Mom or Grandmother ever would have needed backup, which they didn't.

That chair was his comfort sometimes. One day—I don't know why I remember this specifically—he launched himself from the chair and got me, and we went into the backyard. I must have been around ten or eleven. After we finished mowing and raking the yard, he looked down at the rake I had put on the ground, tines up. "You don't want to do that," he said. "Why?" Now, it didn't take a genius to see what he was getting at, and any average kid of my generation had seen enough cartoons to know that a tines-up rake is a joke-grenade ready to go off in someone's face. I was just being annoying and hardheaded because I saw a chance to be.

He stepped on the rake rather gently, and the handle rose toward his face. He let the handle come to near vertical and then put his hand around it, bringing the handle closer to his face to make the point. "See? If you leave the rake lying around like this, someone could step on it and get hit." I said, "You caught it." He sighed, and let the rake down. He stepped on it harder, and it came up to him faster. He caught the rake again, but not so easily. "When you step on it like normal, it's going to come up faster, and hit somebody." "That wasn't so fast." He looked at me, getting tired of children. He dropped the rake and stomped on it, the way only a cartoon character rounding a corner, in a screaming hurry to get that mouse/rabbit/duck/roadrunner would. The handle zoomed at his face, and he stopped it, but just barely; he reflexively jerked his head back away from it. "You see how much this could hurt if somebody stepped on it?" "You still caught it." "That's because I was ready." "I would be ready." He looked at me again, but this time it was different. At the time, I didn't understand this look; it was just how adults looked at me sometimes when they were "losing" arguments with me. But now I know.

I taught a high-school class for a year as part of law school, and I've tutored younger children as well. His look was asking, "What the hell is inside your skull that's trying to pass for a brain, and why is its stupidity being unleashed on me?" The follow-up question to that is "Why can't we just kill you people sometimes?" Since he couldn't just kill me, he surrendered logic to power.

He let the rake fall and turned toward the house, toward his chair. Over his shoulder, he said, "Just don't leave the damn thing around, I don't care why you do it, or how fast you can grab it. Put it in the garage, where nobody can step on it." He said more, but I couldn't hear him because he was mumbling to himself, another trait of his I have carried forward. He went into the house and sat back in the chair, I'm sure to take a minute to try to remember what he thought was so great about grandchildren anyway. He rocked and thought, and I imagine that, after a little bit, he forgot what he was so upset about, watching me play with the dogs, or play ball in the yard. He had decided to teach me yard work and safety. He achieved neither of his goals, but he did show me a patience that I would remind myself of in the future, with my students. One day, if I'm lucky, I'll be that exasperated with my grandchildren. After I debate the merits of their existence, I hope I remember the day he and I did this dance. I hope I smile at the thought, from my chair.

The thing he showed me that is now most pervasive in my life wouldn't be relevant until nearly a decade later. He had a cosmetic mirror, a good one with a light and a curvature that made your face huge. He'd sit in his chair, at the kitchen table, leaning forward into the mirror, and pick ingrown hairs from his neck and cheek with a pair of tweezers. Like most black families I knew, we ate off that table: the living room might as well have been bricked off from the house, as much as we used it. I realize now how disgusting it was to have him doing that at the table, but at the age when I first watched him do this, I still considered well-textured mud an occasional taste treat. By the time I was old enough to be grossed out, the ritual just was, like wearing pants. And, anyway, him doing that was fun enough to me, because I'd play with the mirror when he left it on the table. I could never figure out what he was doing with the tweezers, though, besides pulling his face into funny shapes.

When I joined the Army in 1987 and discovered razor burn, mirrors and tweezers became a part of my life ritual, too. He had taught me a black-man thing. I think of my grandfather sometimes as I look into the mirror, fighting with my self-destructive nature. We black warriors battle to keep ourselves from ourselves every day, and that ritual is frustrating. Success for us is so often measured in how little we fail, rather than how much we achieve. Watching us fight can also be beautiful. The beauty is that we still get up to go at it the next day. He showed me that.

Finally, he taught me regret.

Toward the end of his life, he had to leave the chair. He stayed in his bedroom, across the hall, which was on a diagonal line of sight from his bed to mine. He'd had a stroke, and couldn't hold his right hand still. He was tired all the time. My grandmother and mother worked all day, then came home and worked nearly nonstop until late evening, much of the time caring for his basic needs. He and my grandmother had separate bedrooms. Although I know and I'm sure he knew at the time that they loved him, looking back on it, I don't know if anyone really talked to him much anymore. I think he was very bored, during the times that he wasn't occupied by suffering. And even though he was seriously ill, that's a long time to be alone.

I was at the stage in which I was discovering my need for "privacy," and it bothered me that he would watch me in my room. This was after I wanted privacy, but before I had the courage to shut the door. I remember one day I got mad and said to him, "Why are you watching me?" I don't remember what he said back, but it wasn't much. He didn't tell me, "I am a man in his last year of life, dying from cancer and a stroke, stuck in a bed, and what else am I supposed to look at?" He didn't say, "I'm old and I'm watching a boy who looks like me run around my house and put comic-book pictures on my doors, and track dirt on a rug my wife and daughter like but I hate, and I'm remembering watching that boy break my eggs while learning to cook, and I'm remembering him not learning to put a rake away right." He didn't say, "What about the Rainbow Sherbet at United Dairy Farmers, and since it's all I can do, why would you take it away from me, ungrateful, shortsighted, mean boy?" He didn't say any of that, but he could have, he should have.

My family taught me to do my best and then have few regrets. I was wrong to say that to my grandfather, young or not. Even if it was time to assert my right to privacy, I could have picked more powerful and intrusive "enemies" to fight than an old man at the end of his life. I wish I could apologize to him. I don't know if I believe in an afterlife, and I know I don't believe it's a place where everyone's hanging around waiting for me to come and make amends. I never should have said that to him, and now he's gone, and I wish I could make it better, but I can't.

That incident was probably one of the most vivid markers of his illness, and one of his most vivid memories of me. It was certainly one of his last. He didn't deserve that from me. No one dying does. Whatever he did say back to me, it wasn't the truth, or what I deserved. I regret what I said to him, and now I'm more careful with my words, especially in anger. He showed me that, even if what's said is honest, or excusable, you may not be able to take it back if it hurts people, no matter how badly you need to. Their pain is out there, beyond your reach to pull in and take away. But not beyond your memory of causing the pain. That's what regret is: a selfish desire fulfilled, and a need to heal forever denied.

I'm writing this during my last year of law school. I'm twenty-eight and looking forward to becoming a man next year. Manhood has changed some since his day. But I remember what he showed me. I remember him through the older people, in their eyes, like fading starlight. But I also remember him directly.

Grandfathers

🎑🎑🎑

Ashley Bryan

My parents' fathers died when they were young so I did not know my grandparents. The man I've pictured here is George Weston, a family friend from Antigua, who became a grandfather to me.

My parents came to the United States from Antigua in the West Indies after the First World War. They settled in New York City, and their six children were all born and reared in New York. In my family the children called my parents' friends Aunt and Uncle, so I have no problem in thinking of Mr. Weston as Grandfather.

As the years passed I grew close to Mr. Weston. He had been active in the Marcus Garvey movement and spoke of the ideals of the movement throughout his life. In conversation I was held not only by his wide-ranging thoughts but also by his refined manner of speech. He made frequent references to his readings in black history and often emphasized a point in discussion by saying "Know your history!"

Mr. Weston was truly a grandfather to me, the wise

elder who inspired respect and a love of learning. He nurtured strong roots in black culture, branching from this source to the flowering and the song. I have drawn a child at his side reaching for his storyteller's staff. He willingly passed it on.

Woodcut by ASHLEY BRYAN

Biographies

Kwame Alexander is a poet and the president of Alexander Publishing. He has been represented in many anthologies and has made major television appearances, including *Planet Groove* on BET. He lives in Arlington, Virginia.

Lois Berg: "I was born in August 1944 in Mount Sinai Hospital in New York City. Weekends, my maternal grandparents would take a taxi to my house or ride home with my uncle, who lived right next door. It was during those times, with the family around the dinner table, that I learned who I was. I have never forgotten that." Ms. Berg lives in Blacksburg, Virginia, and heads athletic academic services at Virginia Polytechnic Institute.

Father Joseph Brown is a priest, a musical scholar, and a noted authority on American literature. He lives in Carbondale, Illinois.

Ashley Bryan was born and reared in New York City. He studied art at Cooper Union. He retells and illustrates African tales and illustrates introductory selections from the spirituals and the black American poets. He now lives on the Cranberry Isles, near Acadia National Park in Maine.

Marina Budhos received her M.A. from Brown University and earned a Fulbright Scholarship to lecture in India in 1992. Her latest novel, *The Professor of Light,* was published in the spring of 1999.

Hilbert H. Campbell: Before his recent retirement, Hilbert Campbell taught in the English department at Virginia Polytechnic Institute for thirty years. He is the grandfather of two. Mr. Campbell lives in Blacksburg, Virginia.

Lori Marie Carlson is an author and translator who often deals with Spanish and bilingual texts. Her anthology, *Cool Salsa: Bilingual Poems on Growing Up Latino in America,* was both an *SLJ* Best Book of the Year and an ALA Best Book for Young Adults. She lives in New York City.

Danella Carter is a fiction writer and the author of the healthy soul-food cookbook *Down Home Wholesome.* She currently lives in Rome, Italy.

Pearl Cleage is an Atlanta-based writer whose works include plays, poems, essays, and a novel, *What Looks Like Crazy on an Ordinary Day.*

Eugenia Collier has published creative works and scholarly articles in numerous periodicals. With Richard H. Long, she published an anthology, *Afro-American Writing.* Her stories are collected in *Breeder and Other Stories.* She lives in Baltimore, Maryland, where she was born.

Shannon M. Cotter received her B.S. from Virginia Polytechnic Institute and her M.A. in psychology from Hollins College in Roanoke, Virginia. She has worked with emotionally disturbed children and court-ordered juveniles and is hoping to pursue her doctorate in behavioral medicine. Ms. Cotter lives in Salem, Virginia.

Rita Dove: Former U.S. Poet Laureate Rita Dove has published numerous books, among them the Pulitzer Prize–winning *Thomas and Beulah,* a collection of poems based on the lives of her maternal grandparents. She lives in Charlottesville, Virginia.

Twanda Black Dudley is a public-affairs director and evening host for *Flavors After Dark* at Jazz Flavors 104.1 FM in Atlanta. The single mother of two boys, Devin (ten) and Brian (eight), she is also an ordained minister at New Life Christian Ministry in Riverdale, Georgia.

Mari Evans is an award-winning poet and anthologist. Her musical *Eyes* was based on Zora Neale Hurston's *Their Eyes Were Watching God.* Ms. Evans lives in Indianapolis, Indiana.

Nikky Finney was born in Conway, South Carolina, in 1957, at the mouth of the Atlantic Ocean. An associate professor of creative writing at the University of Kentucky, she is a founding member of the community-based writing collective *The Affrilachian Poets.*

Dolores H. Fridge was born November 13, 1945, in Gary, West Virginia. She attended Winona State Teachers College in Minnesota, where she was the first African-American woman to receive a four-year degree. She taught elementary school in Minneapolis for fourteen years, and was appointed Commissioner of the Minnesota Department of Human Rights in the governor's cabinet in 1996.

Joanne V. Gabbin is a poet and professor at James Madison University, where she heads the Honors Program.

Thomas W. Giovanni is a former columnist with *The Maroon Tiger* and a recent graduate of law school. He lives in New York City.

Consuelo Harris is a native of Danville, Virginia. She is a graduate of Bennett College in Greensboro, North Carolina, and before her retirement was head of the Main Library Children's Department, Cincinnati Public Library. Best of all, she is Asia's grandmother.

Hazel Clayton Harrison was born in the backwoods of Georgia and grew up in the back alleys of Ohio. A graduate of Kent State University, she uses her pen to record the hopes and memories of her people's struggle for freedom. Ms. Harrison currently lives in southern California and is working on her first novel.

Chester Higgins, Jr., is an award-winning photojournalist. He is currently working on an illustrated book about the wisdom of our elders. Mr. Higgins lives in Brooklyn, New York.

Walter J. Leonard is a semiretired educator, having served as professor, dean, and college president. He is a visiting scholar at the Centre for Socio-Legal Studies and a member of Wolfson College of Oxford University, Oxford, England.

Matt Lichtel was born, the youngest of four, in Harrisburg, Pennsylvania, in 1974. He recently graduated from Virginia Polytechnic Institute as an English major. He now attends the same university as a graduate student.

Haki R. Madhubuti is a noted poet and the publisher of Third World Press. He lives in Chicago, Illinois.

Chevis Mitchell is a sixteen-year-old with a big heart who misses his grandfather. He lives in Houston, Texas.

John Noelle Moore, a native Virginian, is a professor of English and education at Purdue University. Until he was seven, he lived at 209 Tanyard Road. He lives in West Lafayette, Indiana.

Opal Moore is a scholar and professor of literature. She lives in West Lafayette, Indiana.

John Murray taught chemistry at Virginia Polytechnic Institute. He has traveled widely. His hobbies include birding, mountaineering, speleology, photography, and wildflowers. He maintains walking trails at Warm Hearth.

Sanjay Nigam, M.D., runs a research lab at Harvard University. His first novel, *The Snake Charmer,* was published in the spring of 1998.

Jonathan Patton is a recent graduate of Virginia Polytechnic Institute, where he excelled in his poetry courses. He lives in Goode, Virginia.

Sterling Plumpp was born on January 30, 1940, in Clinton, Mississippi. Plumpp earned a B.A. from Roosevelt in 1968 in Chicago. He now teaches at the University of Illinois at Chicago Circle. He won the Carl Sandburg Literary Arts Award in 1983, and is the author of *I Must Go, 1982,* and seven other collections.

Chris Raschka was awarded a Caldecott Honor for *Yo? Yes!* His many attention-getting picture books since then include *The Genie in the Jar* (words by Nikki Giovanni), *Mysterious Thelonious,* and *Simple Gifts.* He lives in New York City.

Lydie Raschka, a former elementary-school teacher, has written and published a number of nonfiction articles on parenting. She lives in New York City. This is her first piece to be included in a book.

Nefertitti Rhodes was born and reared in Fresno, California. She attended California State University Fresno, where she obtained her B.A. degree in English. She is currently an active member of the Houston African American Writers' Society. Nefertitti is also the proud mother of a one-year-old son named Jason Houston.

Liz Rosenberg has written over a dozen books and edited two recent collections of poetry for young readers—*Earth-Shattering Poems* and *The Invisible Ladder,* which was a *Hungry Mind* Book of Distinction. She lives in Binghamton, New York.

Leo Kamell Sacks is a freelance record producer. His compilations include *The Philly Sound: Kenny Gamble, Leon Huff & the Story of Brotherly Love,* and *Stealing Home: A Tribute to Jackie Robinson* (Sony/Legacy). His contemporary productions for Honey Darling Records include *A Taste of Heaven* by the New Orleans gospel artist Raymond Myles and *Disposable* by the New York pop trio Astro Chicken.

Staci Shands is a soror of Delta Sigma Theta and a public-relations professional. She lives in Jamaica, New York.

Nancy E. Slocum taught history at the University of Maryland and worked in publications and exhibit planning at the Interpretive Design Center of the National Park Service. Her interests include wildflower gardening, canoeing, and reading.

Jessie Carney Smith is university librarian and Camille Cosby Professor at Fisk University. A graduate of North Carolina Agricultural and Technical State, Michigan State, and Vanderbilt universities, and the University of Illinois, she is the author of many important books, including *Epic Lives, Powerful Black Women, Black Firsts, Black Heroes,* and the award-winning *Notable Black American Women.*

Elizabeth Spencer was born in Colorado in 1924. She married in 1948 and had four children. She has lived in Virginia for twenty-five years, and has master's degrees in nursing and gerontology. She taught for fifty-one years, and has been writing for fifteen.

Barbara J. Stevenson is a sixth-grade teacher of math, science, and social studies at McCulloch Middle School in Marion, Indiana, the city in which she was born. Barbara recently completed the first phase of an oral-history project on African Americans in Grant County, including information that dates back to the early 1800s.

Karla Farmer Stouse is working on her first novel while accepting the responsibilities of a writing laboratory. She lives in Sheridan, Indiana.

Vivian E. Timmerman is a lifelong learner and educator interested in history, genealogy, family, reading, making new friends, quilting, and travel. Recreational writing has been a new, enjoyable, stimulating venture for her in her waning years.

Ed Vaughn is a Michigan state representative. He was born in Abbeville, Alabama, and reared in Dothan, Alabama. After earning his B.A. in history at Fisk University, he attended the University of Illinois School of Law. The owner of Vaughn's Bookstore, America's oldest black-owned bookstore, he is married and has six children and seven grandchildren.

Gertrude Weissenborn was born and reared in Minnesota. She is a graduate of Bethany Lutheran College in Mankato, Minnesota. She taught school and married Otto Weissenborn, her former teacher. She says her greatest accomplishment was having two children.

Christopher Whaley, a spoken-word artist at Houston's Mahogany Café, is completing his first volume of poetry, *Thoughts of a Renaissance Man.*

Margaret Worley: Born August 24, 1909, Margaret Worley earned her bachelor's degree in Social Services. After the death of her husband, Charles Worley, in 1995, she moved to the Warm Hearth community.

Jane Breskin Zalben has written and illustrated more than twenty books, and has received many awards and distinctions, including a Sydney Taylor Honor. She lives in Sands Point, New York.